MICROBIAL MYSTERIES

Also by Millicent Eidson

NOVELS

Anthracis: A Microbial Mystery (Book 1)

Borrelia: A Microbial Mystery (Book 2)

Corona: A Microbial Mystery (Book 3)

Dengue: A Microbial Mystery (Book 4)

SHORT WORKS

Red Thread

Monuments: A Ten-Minute Play

Pariah

MICROBIAL MYSTERIES

A Story Collection

Millicent Eidson

Maya Maguire Media - Vermont

Published in North America by Maya Maguire Media, PO Box 1214, Burlington, Vermont 05402; drmayamaguire@gmail.com.

Discover other publications at Maya Maguire Media
https://drmayamaguire.com

FIRST EDITION
ISBN // 978-1-955481-11-3 // PAPERBACK

This book is intended for an adult audience, and may contain language, characters, themes, and content that are offensive or triggering to some readers. Generative artificial intelligence (AI) was not used to write the stories or create the book cover, and use of the text or cover for AI models is prohibited.

Cover bacteria: https://phil.cdc.gov/Details.aspx?pid=23251
Maya Maguire Media logo photo:
https://phil.cdc.gov/Details.aspx?pid=2871

Some stories have been modified by the author from previous releases in literary journals and web magazines, but all rights were retained by the author.

Dedication

Champlain College and the
University of Vermont Writing Programs

Praise for Millicent Eidson

"Millicent Eidson's unparalleled talent shines through in this remarkable work, ensuring a thrilling reading experience. I confidently predict that this offering will be warmly embraced by the literary world, solidifying Millicent Eidson's place among the most esteemed authors of our time."—Midwest Book Review, *Anthracis: A Microbial Mystery*

"Dr. Eidson's medical thriller serves up unique and carefully drawn characters, fascinating and chillingly realistic threats, and enough Happily For Now resolutions to satisfy any women's fiction or romantic suspense fan. You won't want to miss this new entrant into the genre."—Amazon Reviewer, *Anthracis: A Microbial Mystery*

"This 2nd book in the Maya Maguire series follows the intrepid CDC veterinary detective as she tries to track down the mysterious tick microbes causing *Borrelia* infections. Her travels lead her from her home in New Mexico to the European sites of other outbreaks. Meanwhile, Maya is dealing with her own professional and romantic issues. This is a fascinating insider's look at the increasingly menacing diseases arising from animal microbes worldwide."—Amazon Reviewer, *Borrelia: A Microbial Mystery*

"The author's background as a scientist working for the CDC gives you an insider's view of this public-health agency at a time of crisis. I recommend Corona to all fans of medical mysteries."—Amazon Reviewer, *Corona: A Microbial Mystery*

"The mystery, the characters, the setting, and the uncanny timing of this book make it a compelling read. I would recommend it to anyone who loves medical thrillers, mysteries set in Hawaii, mysteries with diverse characters, books with a strong female protagonist, and fictional tales related to climate change."—A.M. Reade, USA Today Bestselling Author, *Dengue: A Microbial Mystery*

TABLE OF CONTENTS

El Chinche

This story is modified from a 2021 release in "Danse Macabre." It is a novel prequel introducing two key public health supervisors, Nancy Bingham and Fred Grinwold. "El Chinche" received an award in 2020 from the Arizona Mystery Writers.

Nogales, Mexico—Tuesday October 12, 1993

Feathery feet and a crepitus body slide across my left eyelid. My palm scrapes blue eyeshadow to the creamy pillowcase, plus an inch-long black-and-gold psychedelic bug which scurries away on jointed legs. A Halloween horror, two weeks early.

Blurry vision of the arresting creature is a clue my debauched night was a disaster. Its larger cousin creeps along my left thigh— while thrusting my leg in the air to dislodge it, I bump the naked backside of the man next to me.

He's pudgy, white, with hairy limbs and a smooth back. A sledgehammer pounds from my eyes to the nape of my neck. Trapped against the copper-hued wall, I slither across him, bare skin rubbing, as my stomach lurches. After tripping over the rug, I crawl into the mosaic bathroom and lose all those glorious salt-rimmed margaritas. Guaymas shrimp—I taste those coming back up, too.

As I crouch on the blue-and-white flowered tiles, fingers stroke my short hair. My head arches up, and I recognize him.

"You okay?" His bulging brown eyes are concerned, but meander in his typical distracted and disinterested way. Under the dark hair, too much minutiae dances through his prodigious brain. I'm sure he really cares.

"Fred, can you help me up?" After he reaches to grip my arm, I lean over the terracotta sink and rinse the yellow-green bile away.

"Get yourself together." The deep voice barks from the bed as he tugs on blue boxers and rumpled tan pants. "We're late for the lead poisoning talk."

For him, the Tuesday morning session of the regional border health meeting is more urgent than washing up. We'll learn about maquiladoras, Mexican factories with insufficient pollution control. But I'm not showing up without a shower.

He's gone when I towel off from the tepid but reviving spray. I step into a satin skirt and pull on a matching blazer. Stand out in a crowd—that's my modus operandi. Although we didn't make the best decisions last night, I was smart enough to have our reunion sex in my hotel room, not his.

A quick blast from the hair dryer on my mousy, brown locks and I'm ready. After riding the creaky elevator to the first floor, at the front desk I call out, "Buenos días, ¿cómo estás?" to la chica bonita, her head crowned by glossy black braids woven with white silk ribbon. As I smile, the wrinkles around my eyes reflect almost thirty years of hot Texas sun. She replies, "Muy bien, ¿y tú?" She has a decade before men start seeing right through her.

I'm not late. Dr. Gonzalez, the Arizona State Epidemiologist, hobnobs in the ballroom with his Sonoran counterpart. My position as a public health physician started three months ago when I finished the Baylor family medicine residency. It's an inspiring time—President Clinton appointed the first African-American director of the Centers for Disease Control and Prevention.

The annual neighbor-state gathering is on the Mexican side this year. Until the difficult dawn, I embraced my first visit to Nogales, Sonora. The temperature hit eighty yesterday, and music spilled out of las cantinas when we strolled for lunch and dinner. Our hosts are relaxed, gregarious, and gracious. The schedule allows time to shop for artesanías—I've a yen for Huichol yarn paintings.

Last month, a highlight of the Puerto Vallarta rabies meeting was the night excursion to capture vampires as they darted in to suck blood from the legs of cattle. Jalisco veterinarians pried the bats out of fence nets and wiped warfarin on their backs. In the roosts, bats rub the paste on their relatives and they bleed out, dying before they can spread rabies. Sounds barbaric, but it reduces vampires feeding on the toes of sleeping people who suffer horrific foaming-at-the-mouth death.

By the time translators don their headsets and everyone settles down, Fred plops on the empty seat beside me. He's in his Public Health Service dress blues—went to his room to change. At the midmorning break, he seizes my forearm, steering me away from the snacks and posters.

"Nancy, I don't regret getting carried away after the banquet. Seven years since we were together, but I never stopped thinking about you."

"We're not going to speak here." I slap his hand aside. Dr. Gonzalez frowns when he sees me—am I that hungover? He might suspect my dalliance, due to our raucous toasting and laughing and singing with the mariachis. Staying glued to the boss's side throughout the remaining presentations is the right decision. Fred can do whatever he needs to, by himself, to slake his thirst.

Nogales, Mexico—Friday, October 15, 1993

Measles. Dr. Fred Grinwold, CDC Epidemic Intelligence Service Officer. Final listing on the Friday schedule. After his presentation and questions, he corners me, and I lead him to the elevator. He's taller and heavier—I can't force him to come, but he follows like a pining puppy. Probably shouldn't boss around an officer, but I'm not ceding control again.

Inside the antiquated hotel room, I perch on one of the equipale chairs and gesture for him to do the same. No evidence remains of our carnal tryst. A reviving breeze ruffles white lace curtains and the enticing, warm aroma of corn tortillas floats in.

"We were infatuated—nuts about each other—during your last semester in Texas," I acknowledge with a faint smile.

Then I take charge—rigid posture, tanned face mask, toneless voice. "But you graduated and headed to Albuquerque for med school. You didn't contact me. Now you're the EIS Officer assigned to the New Mexico Health Department."

Putting a coda to the recollection, I salute. "Congratulations."

He bobs his head, vibrating the double chin. Although he's gained weight since we were lovers at Baylor, his IQ, and a few other talents, still attract me.

"Medical training was important to both of us." He pushes the black-framed glasses higher on his bulbous nose. "We're working close by. Can we repeat Monday night, sometime?"

Only a when-it's-convenient sort of thing—my faith says *no way, Jose*. I already need to take Confession, and won't rewrite my life for him. Phoenix is fabulous, including Saturday Camelback Mountain climbs at dawn. As a native Texan, Arizona's dry heat doesn't faze me.

I shift position while changing the topic. "When we woke up Tuesday, I found ginormous, gross insects on my eyelid and thigh. Both areas itch and I'm woozy, even with cooler temps today."

His full lips twist. "My residency was preventive medicine, not clinical practice."

Thick, short fingers trace my eyelids. "Your left one is inflamed. Want an assessment of your leg?"

"Not necessary—checking that myself." No touching there, now that I'm sober, in my right mind.

Another vivid insect scampers across the floor, heading for a crack in the whitewashed bathroom wall. "Hey, that's it—"

He drops a plastic cup over the bug.

"My hero."

He acknowledges the compliment with a thin smile, and stuffs tissues over the insect. "Is this what you saw before?"

After my nod, he stomps for the door. "The manager needs to hear about this."

"Triatomino—el chinche." The forty-something male summoned by the receptionist ducks his head. "Lo siento, doctora."

Fred rubs his pale, balding forehead. "'Chinche' is used for bedbugs, which are much smaller. This might be similar—sucks blood while you sleep."

Like a vampire bat. But I'm lucky—insects don't transmit rabies. My skin starts to tingle. "Creepy to envision it biting me, especially on my eyelid."

"Tape this up, so it won't escape," Fred directs the manager. I'm not used to him being so organized. When the bug is secure, he turns on me. "Meeting's over—you're riding with me to Phoenix."

Darned if he'll order me around like the hired help. "I came with the boss, and will go back that way."

His skin blazes—he pretends to be taciturn but his emotions are clear. The manager's and the receptionist's inky eyes dart between us. Probably wondering who will win out in this gringo battle. After achieving simultaneous agreement not to be hotel entertainment, we migrate toward the ballroom.

"You're on my route to Santa Fe." He lifts his glasses and scrubs his eyes. "I can't remember if bites from this bug carry any health risk."

I'm embarrassed, too. "Guess we're both green—let's ask Dr. Gonzalez." But everyone's disappeared to the farewell brunch. The blood-sucking insect skittering in the cup kills our appetites.

"Leave him a message," Fred tells me, "and you're going home."

A white vintage Corvair idles near the sliding door when I check out and leave a note summarizing the change of plans. Despite the brisk draft through the lobby, hot flashes prickle my skin while I whisper a sentimental adiós to dozens of rustic whiskey barrels overflowing with spectacular, multicolored annuals.

I toss my luggage into Fred's back seat and needle him about the car. "Unsafe at any speed."

"Ralph Nader be damned—this is my baby. Named her Ethyl."

At the border, an American officer glances at Fred's license and waves us through. Crossing south on Monday morning, the Mexican guard hesitated until my boss pulled out a twenty to cover both of us. La Mordida—the bite. Price to avoid a delaying inspection.

"Any guess when we'll get to Tucson?" The interstate isn't finished and travel is slow in spots. I'm flushed and faint. Nobody on the planet gets more car sick as a passenger—that's all it is. As I doze off, I discern an answer, but it doesn't register.

Fists of hail strike the front windshield and rock me out of my reverie. Fred swerves over to an ocotillo-thatched ramada protecting a concrete picnic table. Wind whips the thin green palo verde branches and the thicker dark mesquites.

"We're close to Tubac and Presidio ruins, but today's not ideal for sightseeing. How are you doing?"

Although tucked off the road, the Corvair frame is light, like Nader warned, twitching with every gale gust. Through the car vents, bursts of chilly air waft my favorite bouquet of desert-after-a-rain, but my epidermis breaks out with goosebumps and my limbs shake.

Fred reaches back and unhooks the latches on the sparkly pink hard-covered suitcase. He rumples through everything, including underwear, until he discovers my bulky Irish wool sweater. Before pulling it over my head, he caresses my neck and forehead.

"You've got a fever and the inflammation of your left eyelid is expanding."

No joke—my vision is narrowed. So I don't catch him reaching for my skirt before he yanks it up. "Hell of a rash."

I glance down at my baby's-flesh upper thigh. The discolored area is extensive, round, and pearlescent red. "Guess I need to brush up on bug-borne diseases." My pronouncement slips out, barely audible.

He twists the ignition key and burns rubber back to the highway. "We're stopping at the University of Arizona Hospital."

As he carries me into the ER, my eye is swollen shut and my head vibrates like our morning after. I'm short of breath when adjusting my position on the gurney. And my heart's racing—I hate being out of the loop while Fred pulls out el chinche and discusses it with the lab attendant.

After they take blood and urine specimens, and run an EKG, a compact Native American stops by.

"Dr. Bingham? I'm Louis Lopez, chief resident. Dr. Grinwold gave us the triatomine from your hotel. People call them kissing bugs, because they bite faces. Arizona Poison Control gets more calls about them than anywhere in the country. Pima County is the hotspot—about forty percent of the bugs here have *Trypanosoma cruzi*, which causes Chagas Disease."

Fred's voice is tentative. "Wouldn't you feel the bite? We were, um, together when Nancy found them on her."

Lopez is professional and doesn't remark on the personal reveal. "They suck blood for half an hour if someone is a heavy sleeper or somehow impaired."

Yeah, somehow impaired.

"Human cases are a mystery in the US. You'll be the first I've diagnosed, if confirmed."

My synapses kick in. "Protozoan parasite, squiggly little worm. Sorry, not you Fred. The parasite."

From the grim expressions, I notice neither is amused. "Anyone looking at my blood smear?"

Lopez nods. "Eye swelling is called Romaña sign. Can happen from the bug bite, without *T. cruzi* transmission."

His fingers rub my neck below the ear, and I flinch. Doctors shouldn't show pain.

"Left superficial cervical lymph node is enlarged."

He must be afraid I'm not sufficiently worried because his voice turns harsh. "Ten to forty percent of cases develop cardiovascular and gastrointestinal complications. Repeat bites can kill instantly from anaphylaxis."

Fred plonks down, clutching my hands. Basset hound eyes— comforting. I tilt in his direction, easing the left-sided discomfort. My right eye closes to match the other one, and I drift away.

Tucson, Arizona—Saturday, October 16, 1993

Lopez reappears with a gray-haired woman trailing. "I hate to start off your weekend with such bad news," he says. "Your bug has the parasite and you have Chagas."

Fred's massive dome jerks up. Huddled at the bedside all night—what a sweetheart.

I locate Lopez with my operational eye. "Transmitted through the bite?"

"Grosser than that—the bug contaminates bite wounds, or conjunctivae of the eyes, with its feces."

The older lady steps forward. "I'm Edith Nichols with the Arizona-Sonora Desert Museum. We want to compare with Sonora our Pima County insects and animal hosts, like armadillos, opossums, or wood rats. Did you spy any of those species on the hotel grounds?"

"Your point." Fred is rude and impatient—what else is new?

"Our bugs are springtime—warmer temps, drier—but the weather's been similar this month, unusually hot. We research climate change on species, and want to be in synch with President Clinton's Climate Change Action Plan."

Fred's weight shifts—he emanates intimidating vibes. Ms. Nichols glances at her watch and reaches out to him. "Here's my card."

After her exit, Lopez reviews my chart. "You're a big deal—scientists are fascinated."

"I'll handle the Museum." Despite the disheveled uniform, Fred maintains his no-nonsense CDC persona. "What's the treatment plan?"

"Dr. Bingham has some early anomalies including sinus tachycardia. A cardiologist is coming to consult. We'll start nifurtimox for ninety days—not FDA-approved, but we have no risk-free options."

He hands me a xerox. "Medication side effects include depression, insomnia, and memory loss. Take this seriously—chronic neurologic and cardiac complications could show up in twenty years, and be fatal. Ten thousand deaths a year worldwide—that's the estimate."

He scrutinizes Fred. "One more thing."

Then the black eyes pin me. "I could order a pregnancy test—fetal transmission can cause microencephaly or death."

Shit.

If Chinche isn't a Spanish swear word, it should be. I'm a semi-good Catholic girl and responsible doc—we used protection, didn't we?

SARS

This is another Nancy Bingham/Fred Grinwold prequel for the alphabetical novels, never previously released.

Prologue: Spillover

Leaps from animals to humans—a zoonotic spillover. Coronaviruses used to stick to their own kind, their animal reservoirs. Invading the cells, taking control, making the host do its bidding by churning out virus replicas.

But corona is restless, ever mutating, seeking any evolutionary advantage. Humans and their airplanes—a felicitous target.

Chapter One

Glenwood, New Mexico—Sunday, March 23, 2003

The dark metal railing pressed into Nancy's lower back, cushioned by the fluorescent pink daypack, as Fred leaned down for the kiss. In one hand, she held his black-framed glasses, and the other encircled his weightlifter neck. Cool spring air under the cliff overhang counteracted the heat of their ardor as tumbling waterfalls eclipsed most other sounds.

He grabbed back his glasses and scrambled for the Blackberry in the holster on his waist. "Not me, must be you."

"Surprised you could hear anything over the din of Whitewater

Creek." She reached around to tug her pack forward and unzipped the small front pocket covered with souvenir patches from trips to Mexico, Alaska, and Hawaii. "Amazing that a signal got through this deep in the canyon."

But the attempt to return the phone call on her own Blackberry didn't work. She pressed the small, raised buttons below the black-and-white screen to open up emails, then read aloud. **"Suspect SARS. Can you consult with Safford Hospital?"**

Fred frowned and arched his neck to read over her shoulder. "Severe acute respiratory syndrome? I saw the CDC report of eleven US cases, but this would be the first from our area."

As a family of three joined them, Fred guided Nancy closer to the rough rock wall. The woman pulled the young girl back from red-and-white boulders scattered in the creek's tumbling foam like giant toy blocks.

"Dr. Gonzalez should handle something this high profile," Fred said in Nancy's ear. "I'd take care of it myself if the case was here in New Mexico."

She swatted an annoying horsefly and headed down the trail. "Don't be dissing my boss. Safford's on my way back to Phoenix. The patient's a young Mormon missionary in critical condition."

The view of rushing water below the hanging bridge didn't deter her step. She trusted in the wire mesh despite Fred's heavy weight. For the return mile, alternating rocky dirt path, cement paved sections, and metal catwalks, she led the way. Overhanging maples provided brief breaks from late March sunrays piercing the narrow slot canyon at noon.

As they approached giant Arizona sycamores that shaded the picnic area near the parking lot, massive bolts dotted the canyon wall to keep it from disintegrating onto the trail in a rock fall. With the temperature in the seventies, children screamed and splashed through the gurgling brook under a cottonwood canopy. The canyon walls opened up, speckled with low piñons and junipers.

Nancy stopped in front of Fred's dusty white Corvair. "Thanks for sharing New Mexico mining history." She glanced around the parking lot empty of people and lowered her hand to the front of his pants. "And last night at Glenwood Inn."

He groaned as he stroked the yellow fabric of her short jumper, now dusted with artsy red spots. "So why aren't we staying one more night? Gonzalez never gets off his lazy ass to take care of anything himself."

Her fingers drifted past the Zia sun symbol belt buckle to his denim front pocket and removed his car key. "You're jealous he beat you out two years ago to become CSTE President."

"Rub it in, why don't you? It's the Council of State and Territorial Epidemiologists. No mention of cities. So why is that NYC vet Faye Simpson his successor? She's just a dog catcher."

Nancy shouldered him aside to open his driver's side door. "I don't like your beef with vets in public health, especially women. Your fellow State Epidemiologists elected her, so she must be a dynamo."

He kissed her nose as he flashed a conciliatory smile. "If the Big Apple needs a vet to handle their animal bites, more power to them. But how in hell will she manage our interests when she takes over CSTE?"

"You'll be preoccupied planning the huge fortieth birthday party you promised me in the fall." She patted him on the rear of his relaxed-fit pants. "Meanwhile you can gloat that you won't hit that milestone for a whole nuther year."

He held her tight in a farewell bear hug. "Never going to let me forget your superior maturity, are you?"

Nancy broke his grip and headed for her F-150 pickup. "In your dreams. Duty calls—I'll check in later. Luv ya!" She rolled down the window, slid into the hot seat, and slipped Lyle Lovett's *Pontiac* into the CD player to blare "She's No Lady" as her tires kicked up dirt.

Within an hour, the two-lane highway crossed into Arizona through small hills punctuated by carpet swatches of evergreen junipers and piñons. East of Safford, the terrain flattened into dusty fields. Soon, they'd be dotted with monster green trucks trailing multiple rakes to plant cotton seed. Nancy sighed in contentment, brushing bangs out of her eyes. She never tired of the view from the high seat of the Ford truck during her field trips throughout the expansive state of Arizona, or the decade of jaunts to reconnoiter with Fred in New Mexico.

Inside the one-story cement block hospital, she was greeted by the director, a stooped octogenarian who introduced himself as Bruce Oswald.

"Nancy Bingham?" He fiddled with his hearing aids. "Dr. Gonzalez said you were on your way. I've lived and worked here for fifty years without a puzzle like this."

Beaming a broad smile, she shook his hand. "Dr. Oswald, I admire your dedication on a Sunday. Not sure I'll be able to keep all this up when I'm your age."

He winked a heavily creased eyelid. "Someone young and energetic like you can do anything she wants. I'm glad Alejandro asked you to stop by in person."

Self-conscious of her hours hiking, she glanced to her dusty calves and pink tennis shoes. "I've been to the Glenwood Catwalk. Can I clean up before we see your patient?"

The doctor's voice was throaty and cheerful, despite his perplexing case. "Of course, my dear. A changing room is around the corner. Meet you inside when you're ready."

Nancy showered for less than two minutes and donned a surgical gown, then finished with paper coverings for her head and feet, adding a mask, gloves and goggles. In the ICU room, the blond patient was pale and unconscious, his breathing assisted by a ventilator. Short in stature but well-muscled, he could have been a teen gymnast. But despite his youth, the hands on the sheet looked like her father's, calloused from ranch work.

"Ammon Musser, age twenty," Dr. Oswald said. "He's been on a Mormon mission to Hong Kong, which has been a SARS hotspot. He assisted with hotel religious services for Latter-day Saints women from other countries who are nannies, cooks, or housecleaners."

Nancy pulled her Blackberry from her pocket. "Are you familiar with CDC's *Morbidity and Mortality Weekly Report?* The *MMWR*s are always released on Friday." She tried to show him the tiny Blackberry screen. "It mentions two hundred sixty-four suspect or probable cases worldwide so far, most of them in Hong Kong."

Dr. Oswald squinted at her hand. "Your gadget's not easy on the eyes. Can you send the report? Your boss said we should review Ammon's illness to see if it could be SARS."

"CDC has the preliminary case definition right here. Does Ammon have a fever?"

A tiny nurse, looking no older than Ammon, piped up. "102.3 degrees. He's been febrile for the four days since he flew back. Normally they can't come home during the two years of the mission, but his father died in a freak accident last week, so they approved Ammon's return for the funeral. His family's in Thatcher."

Nancy scribbled notes with red ink in her purple pocket notebook. "Sounds like the family can't get a break."

As the nurse checked the intravenous fluid line, Dr. Oswald answered. "We admitted Ammon Friday night for an alarming struggle to breathe and severe diarrhea."

He pointed to the chest x-ray film hanging in front of a light box, showing whited out lungs replacing normal black air-filled spaces. "With radiographic confirmation of pneumonia, we considered plague and hantavirus, but those are rare here in the southern part of the state. Initial tests came back negative, and I heard about the SARS report, so I called your office."

Nancy lifted Ammon's eyelid to verify the yellowing of his eyes. The young nurse chimed in. "He has elevated liver enzymes."

The door eased open as a salt-and-peppered head leaned in. "Dr. Oswald, Ammon's mother returned from the father's graveside after the funeral service. The rest of the family is at the mercy meal. She'd like to visit."

"Can she hang on a minute?" Nancy glanced at Ammon's immobile body with mechanical support keeping him alive. She hated separating a mother from her desperately-ill child, but wearing her public health hat, a confirmatory diagnosis was essential. "With his travel history, he could be our first case of SARS. It's a brand new disease, and we don't know how to help him. I'll call CDC for specimen collection instructions."

Dr. Oswald checked the vitals on the video screen next to the bed. "Patients don't have a promising prognosis on a ventilator long-term."

"WHO guidance mentioned combining ribavirin intravenously with high-dose corticosteroids. Antibiotics don't appear to help."

"Yes, his diarrhea has worsened, so we'll stop those on your recommendation."

Nancy wrinkled her nose under the mask, recognizing the odor the nurses struggled to keep under control.

Dr. Oswald tilted his face closer. "Any changes to our personal protective equipment?"

Nancy scanned her screen. "Secondary attack rates are more than fifty percent in healthcare workers caring for Hong Kong and Hanoi patients. With these N95 respirator masks and eye protection, you've got the recommended level of PPE. When the lab confirms the pathogen, I'll ask about additional steps."

The older assistant knocked and opened the door again. "Mom's still waiting."

The woman with light skin marked by tiny crinkles pushed in. Steely blue eyes peered over the mask and a dark blonde bun protruded from the back of the head covering. Nancy grabbed her by the elbow and escorted her back out. "Mrs. Musser? I'm Dr. Bingham from the state health department. Can we talk outside and let the hospital staff care for your son?"

The woman ripped off her gown, exposing a simple black dress extending to the floor. "I don't understand why I can't see him. They let me in yesterday. What's changed?" With the mask and eye protection removed, tears streaked her freckled apple cheeks.

Nancy pulled her down to a chair bolted to the wall outside the ICU room. "I'm so sorry for the loss of your husband, and now Ammon is ill. One family shouldn't have to go through so much. But your faith keeps you strong." She slowed her next words to make sure the woman heard the common Mormon admonition. "You need to choose the right path at this moment."

"I WANT TO SEE HIM." The woman's fingers on Nancy's right wrist pinched like channel-lock pliers.

With a gentle hold on the woman's other hand, Nancy hoped to get through to her. "Our suspicion is a foreign, imported disease. Microbes like hantavirus which aren't spread person-to-person have been ruled out. This could be more dangerous."

Mrs. Musser let go of Nancy and twisted in the seat. "Worse than Navajo flu? Our kinfolk in the north say the death rate is high from that."

Nancy nodded. "This new disease from Hong Kong is called SARS and it appears to be highly contagious. We haven't confirmed what Ammon has, but it's better to be safe. Can you put together a list of everyone near him since he's been home? I'll call you tomorrow, and please minimize contact with other people until we sort this out."

The woman pulled out a white handkerchief from the pocket of her skirt and wiped her streaked cheeks. She gulped rapidly to slow her sobs. "I wanted his mission closer to home, with people like us. Safer."

Nancy tried a different tactic. "I understand—we all want to protect our children."

Mrs. Musser's eyes snapped to Nancy's left hand, free of the gloves. "You're not married, how would you know?"

A sharp pain pinched between Nancy's shoulder blades and her voice hardened like granite. "You're right, becoming a mother isn't in the cards for all of us." Then she took back Mrs. Musser's hands and struggled to avoid lecturing. "As a doctor with the state health department, I view all Arizonans as my children. My life is dedicated to preventing illness. I'm doing everything I can to make sure no one else gets sick."

Chapter Two

Phoenix, Arizona—Monday, March 24, 2003

As the sun pinked up Camelback Mountain, Nancy dawdled over coffee on a wicker chair in the small patio of her graveled backyard. With impatience, she dropped the newspaper trumpeting Operation Iraqi Freedom, worldwide protests, and the deaths of the first Marines. She gazed fondly over the desertscape established with Fred's help ripping out the water-sucking Bermuda grass.

In her only concession to greenery, she'd kept the splashy oleander bushes lining the chain link fence, looming at more than twice her five-foot four inches and providing privacy from the neighbors. The leathery bright green leaves almost blotted out the gray stems, sprouting bouquets ranging from white to yellow to deep crimson. She strolled closer to catch the faint apricot blossom smell but didn't finger the flowers, aware of the plant's toxicity. Everything had its tradeoffs, and not having kids or pets allowed her to surround the yard with walls of beauty harboring hidden poison.

After slipping into a mauve pantsuit, she drove to the office and prioritized cornering her boss. Alejandro Gonzalez was gorgeous and knew it, with constant reminders from his wife that he was her personal Jimmy Smits. But Nancy found him less ingratiating than the actor. Mercurial moods made no difference—she was used to brusque, temperamental men. All their stormy expressions and blaring pronouncements were blown away like a puff of smoke. Her father, the owner of a Texas feed store, had instilled in her an unshakeable confidence, while her stay-at-home mom modeled careful stroking of the male ego.

"So you really think this Mormon kid has a strange, imported disease?" Dr. Gonzalez asked as he reclined in the ancient, padded rocking chair. "Have you talked to the lab? What about influenza or respiratory syncytial virus? *Haemophilus influenzae, Strep pneumoniae,* or *Staph aureus?*"

"Checking with the lab is first on my list. You're right, the only thing tying this patient to SARS is his Hong Kong mission. I'll consult with CDC's State Support Team."

"It's paramount nobody lets this out." Dr. Gonzalez slammed his binder on the ornate oak desk. "I'll hold you personally responsible for press leaks. The family, the hospital, our staff, CDC—nobody talks. It's been a decade since that hantavirus mess. I want things quiet and calm. Let people focus on the search for Saddam."

Like the repeated blares of a train approaching a crossing, every word blasted the walls—ironic that he was so concerned with confidentiality. But she smiled and agreed. He'd been ground beneath the snakeskin boots of the governor before, and she understood his worries.

Phoenix, Arizona—Tuesday, April 1, 2003

A week later when Nancy called the elderly Safford hospital director, he sounded like a bullfrog.

"Our hospital's got an increase in people coughing," he said. "Mine's only a cold, but I'm worried about some of the others."

"Did you ban all nonessential staff members and visitors like I recommended after talking to CDC?"

"Yes, we're a tight ship. Those needing outpatient or elective inpatient care are sent to Tucson. It's a major burden for them, but we're following your guidance."

"Is Ammon still recovering at home? It's a miracle he regained consciousness and was discharged within a week, especially since we're not sure of his diagnosis. You must have a remarkable level of care out there in cotton country. Or Angel Moroni is watching out for him."

"Ammon's fine with supplemental oxygen and supremely happy in the bosom of his extended family. I'm guessing the methylprednisolone helped him turn the corner. Hey, did I tell you how Ammon's father died?"

"You said freak accident."

His chuckle was interrupted with a short bout of coughing. "Cactus plugging—shooting holes in saguaros—is an occasional pastime in these parts. He knocked off a mammoth arm which crushed him.”

She was tempted to search her computer to see if he was kidding. But then she remembered the song *Saguaro* from a Texas band, the Austin Lounge Lizards.

Her April First cartoon-a-day calendar showed a veterinarian in the shape of a cat telling the avian patient perched on the exam table, ‘Gull stones.’ Maybe he was toying with her. “Dr. Oswald, you’re not pulling my leg for April Fool’s, are you?”

“Nope, cosmic joke. Shouldn’t find the humor in it—such a shock to the family.” He coughed again.

“Are you sure you didn’t catch something from Ammon?”

“Low-grade fever and sore throat—happens several times a year. But with others coughing too, can you come down for a consult?”

“Let me talk to Dr. Gonzalez, then I’ll see you at midday.”

Although anxious to reach Safford, she appreciated the stark scenery along the two-lane highway, the most direct route. Passing the Apache Gold Casino, she remembered a Christmas weekend there with Fred several years earlier. She lost more at poker than he thought reasonable, and like a Puritan preacher, he condemned her to hell and froze her out for the next two weeks. It just reinforced their innate differences and her decision to pursue her career in Arizona.

Energized by the dazzling day, she cranked the window open and the radio higher. After replaying Mary Chapin Carpenter’s *Come On Come On* three times, she was belting “He Thinks He’ll Keep Her” at the top of her lungs as she pulled into the hospital parking lot at noon. In Dr. Oswald’s office, his blue veins striped the paper-thin skin of his hands as he swiped at his reddened nose with a tissue. “You’re not looking so hot,” she told him.

“Au contraire, temp’s 100.4, below the cutoff for SARS. Don’t get to my age without a robust immune system.”

She scoffed as she pulled out her stethoscope. “Can we go to an exam room so I can check you over?”

After donning PPE, she asked him to cough as she listened to his lungs and heart. "Sounds dry and nonproductive—could fit with SARS. Had a chest radiograph?"

He patted her gloved hand. "Not that bad, Nancy. But two of my staff are hospitalized."

Insist he get x-rays or isolate? But he was twice her age with years of experience and should know if he was really ill. Having him still functioning was important to her investigation. "Germany and Hong Kong think they found a paramyxovirus so this could be contagious like measles. SARS case fatality rate is currently about three percent, which fits with measles."

He shook his head. "Except we don't have measles. No rash illness."

"Yeah, it's taking a frustrating amount of time to identify new disease agents. If you think you might have an outbreak here at the hospital, I need to interview staff. Can you pull up a list of anyone who worked with Ammon? I'll start with those here, then move onto any of your employees calling in sick."

He led her back to his office to open up the personnel file on his computer. She tugged a heavy ThinkPad from her daypack and inserted a 3.5-inch floppy disk. "If I type out a questionnaire, could someone help administer it?"

"Too short-staffed at the moment and I need to check on patients. Can Dr. Gonzalez assist?"

"No problem. I'll take care of my calls outside on this gift-from-God day."

At a bench overlooking the greening swale of the Gila River, she inhaled the sweet smell of alfalfa, wafting over from the windrower trucks clipping the top growth from fall planting. The odor triggered early childhood reflections on her family's verdant Brazos Valley farm before they were forced out by De Cordova Bend Dam.

After her grandfather offered his son-in-law a feedstore job almost five hundred miles southwest, her wanderings switched from catching crawdads to chasing horny toads through prickly pear cacti. The pain of their loss was retriggered with the Baylor English class requiring the John Graves book *Goodbye to a River*.

The first phone call from her Blackberry failed to garner support. Dr. Gonzalez was tied up in a meeting with their health director, so she punched in the number to Santa Fe. "Hey Fred, knock knock."

A deep sigh and a door closing. "I'll play along, who's there?"

Why did his staff find him so humorless? She always knew how to arouse his cuddly koala side. "Int."

"I'll never guess this. Say it again."

Her pronunciation was loud and deliberate. "I-N-T. Int."

The second sigh was a hair more exasperated. "Int who?"

"Into my private parts is where I want you to be . . . except I might have to break my promise of visiting New Mexico. I'm back in Safford for a possible outbreak related to our suspect SARS case."

Was his grumpy groan for the joke or jeopardizing plans for a weekend concert? But he knew that a nosocomial outbreak, spread of disease within a hospital, required immediate investigation.

"It's only Tuesday, so I might finish in time to join you in Santa Fe Saturday morning."

She spotted the hospital director waving from the employee entrance. "Sorry, sweetie, gotta go, but I'll keep you posted."

As Dr. Oswald held the door open, he gave her an update. "Carol Russell is one of our ill staff. She was the admitting doc for Ammon a week ago Friday. With her asthma, she's taken a turn for the worse, and we're moving her to the ICU now."

Safford, Arizona—Friday, April 4, 2003

After three nights in a Safford motel nestled in a pecan grove next to the river, Nancy had completed follow-up on anyone at the hospital with respiratory signs and their contacts. She spied Dr. Oswald outside Dr. Russell's ICU room and handed him pages generated from her portable printer. "This is the latest *MMWR* from CDC, plus my notes from interviews with seven possible SARS patients. Our small cluster is similar to the nationwide trends."

In addition to Ammon, the southeastern Arizona suspect cases included Dr. Russell and a respiratory therapist, the young nurse Nancy had met with Ammon, his mother, and two younger siblings. Her boss ignored her requests for assistance and messages went to voicemail. He was always tied up with their director on some unknown emergency. When his secretary cornered him, he called with marching orders.

"Make those hicks fall in line," he shouted. "If not hospitalized, I want every suspect case isolated at home for ten days. Last thing I need is for Arizona to be the US hotspot, bandied about in the international news like Hong Kong."

His booming voice had no effect on her mood but she'd follow his orders. When raised poor in the Texas badlands, you learned to roll with the punches. Boys will be boys, and she understood from her dad's struggles that bluster often covered insecurity.

"I'm so relieved we didn't have to intubate her." Dr. Oswald's blue eyes were bloodshot as he gazed through the ICU room window at the overweight mid-fifties woman in an oxygen mask. Although pale and grasping the nurse's hand with only two fingers, she chatted in a low voice, her facial expression animated. The nurse nodded and rotated Dr. Russell's body to the right, then applied ointment to a reddened bedsore on the back of her upper left thigh.

"Carol would rather be put down like a horse than incapacitated and unable to speak," Dr. Oswald joked. "We've tested her and the other suspects for everything—*Mycoplasma*, *Chlamydia*, and a gift basket crammed full of viruses. Nothing's popping up on throat swabs, sputum, blood samples, or urine."

Worried about his tottering frail frame, Nancy guided him down to the plastic molded chairs. "If it's any comfort, we're small potatoes. Suspect case count in the US is about a hundred, out of two thousand worldwide. And the American patients are mostly recovering without any antiviral treatment."

"Ten days of isolation for the Mussers could be tough." Then his downturned lips relaxed into a smile. "But I'm forgetting—LDS families are prepared for emergencies with food storage."

She patted his arm. "Don't worry, I've been monitoring them by phone, but I'll drive out there this afternoon. Ten-day isolation is reasonable based on the period people need to watch for symptoms if arriving in the US on flights from Southeast Asia."

Dr. Oswald stood again to peer in at his colleague, now dozing. "Sure wish CDC or the state lab had nailed down the culprit." He glanced quickly over the *MMWR*. "First you were telling me a possible paramyxovirus, but this mentions metapneumovirus and coronavirus."

Nancy pulled her keys from her pocket. "You've got things under control. Half of community-acquired pneumonia cases never have an infectious organism identified. Only thing unusual here is Ammon's travel from Hong Kong. I'll make sure all's AOK with the Mussers in Thatcher."

She gave him a warm hug, relieved his cough had resolved and he wasn't one of the suspect cases. "Dr. Oswald, who takes care of you? I know you're a workaholic widower. Please get some lunch and an afternoon nap. You're the boss—delegate."

Her truck crossed the wide drainage of the Gila River twice on the ten-mile trip through downtown Safford and Thatcher to the cluster of Mormon family farms. The water level was low and didn't fill the channel. But Dr. Oswald said that flash floods in prior monsoons had wiped away half of the Musser's land.

After stepping out of the truck, she found the recovering missionary relaxing under the branches of a weeping willow, body slouched on the rusty metal lawn chair and bare toes curled in the warm grass.

"Hi Ammon, I'm Dr. Bingham from state health. I visited when you were on the ventilator. Glad to see you're off the oxygen and enjoying this delightful spring afternoon."

His face looked younger than his twenty years. "Yeah, I only need it now to help me sleep. Mom's taking a nap. The little kids, they wear her out."

"Your brothers who are sick, where are they?"

"Grandma's got 'em next door."

"Have you heard about a similar illness in your Hong Kong colleagues?"

"I'm the only one who came home, 'cause of my dad."

"I was so sorry to hear about your father. Sudden death is such a shock, especially at a young age. I'm glad you have such a tight net of family and church support."

As the screen door creaked, she glanced to the house, identifying the blonde head poking through the crack. "Excuse me, Ammon, let me talk with your mom."

When Nancy reached the covered porch with torn screens, Ammon's mother dropped to a peeling white swing. Cockroaches scurried for the concrete foundation cracks as the woman's slippered feet skimmed the blue-painted floor.

"Mrs. Musser, how are you feeling?" Nancy knew her role wasn't clinical, but her family practice training kicked in.

The woman coughed and barely got a hand to her mouth before coughing again. "A bit chilled with the fever, and glad my Ma has the other kids."

Nancy stayed close to the screen door but donned a mask from her pack even though they were outside and the woman wasn't ill enough to be hospitalized. "Still have help monitoring your clinical condition?"

Mrs. Musser nodded. "The visiting nurse stops in once a day to check on us and I take hits off Ammon's oxygen machine." She paused, a challenge carved into her freckled face. "Don't report me for that. He doesn't miss it."

"I'm happy he's home with you. I apologize again for restricting entry to his room when we met. Your illness and Ammon's travel from Hong Kong could be unrelated. But it's safer to minimize the contacts any ill family members have until fully recovered, preferably for ten days. Think you can pull that off?"

From the chipped table at her side, the woman poured a glass of sun tea and didn't offer one. With a put-upon friendly tone, her words dripped like the lemon juice she squeezed. "Yeah, doc, we're on top of it." Resentment oozed in a hazy, hot cloud.

Nancy lowered the brim of her red cap, the purple blazer clinging like saran wrap to the bright floral silk blouse. She grew up in a rusted double-wide with an even more colorful variety of roaches, but Mrs. Musser didn't need to know that.

Through the barricade of bushes, Nancy made out a stucco structure closer to the river. "That where Grandma lives?"

A hound-mix bounded up and pushed through the flimsy door to join them. He devoured one of the running roaches before Mrs. Musser said, "Frank, go find Grandma." As Nancy swiveled, uncertain what to do next, the woman added, "Open the door for him. Know how to track an animal?"

Nancy and the dog ducked around a monster castor bean bush with huge lobed leaves, another of the poisonous plants in Arizona masking as deciduous beauty. Ironic that spiny cacti were edible, unlike the oleanders and castor beans that killed if ingested. Frank had his own agenda, sniffing at the ground and stopping to lift a leg at every bush. But the tan house topped by a red metal roof was in sight as her Blackberry chirped and she held it to her ear. The voice of Dr. Gonzalez triggered aural pain.

"Newspaper's running an article about our cluster. Get the fuck back here to handle the interview."

Chapter Three

Phoenix, Arizona—Tuesday, April 8, 2003

"Please locate Ronnie Ibarra," Nancy instructed the front desk through her Blackberry. "Ask her to bring Mr. Bresnitz up here to the conference room." Nancy adjusted her skirt and paced, waiting for the reporter to arrive. Dr. Gonzalez always tightly controlled press contacts, but this time he was AWOL, at a meeting with the Governor.

Usually nothing knocked Nancy back, but she was extra-alert for her first in-person briefing of someone representing the state's largest newspaper. The department's Public Information Officer guided Chuck Bresnitz through the door and pushed coffee and strawberry-iced Krispy Kremes on him like a drug dealer. Ronnie was enough of a Jennifer Lopez lookalike that Nancy counted on her to spin the story in their favor.

Wedged into an armchair at the end of the table, Chuck accepted the PIO's bribes with a broad smile. He and Ronnie had been around the block before on health department news, and she clearly knew what he liked. In his late fifties, Chuck was short and squat, the top of his head gleaming under the ceiling fluorescents. A two-fisted consumer, he juggled cup and pastry with nary a breath between.

Nancy hoped the sugar would lull him into cooperation if he didn't choke first. Fred was balding—would he look like Chuck in another fifteen years? But Fred was more imposing. She had to admit she was attracted to hefty men—got a kick out of pushing them around.

Chuck dropped the goodies with a satisfied sigh to palm a pen and pad. "Dr. Bingham, I hope you appreciate that I sat on this for a few days. When I worked for *Newsday*, that wouldn't have happened. But I escaped that insanity for a more relaxed life, so I'll roll with the mañana mood if it doesn't go much longer."

Nancy joined Ronnie on the charm offensive and tugged on the V-neck of her thin pink sweater. Cleavage never had a downside. With wrinkles already crowding her honeyed eyes, as Fred referred to the ordinary brown color, she used what she could to influence the opposite sex. But Chuck's eyes drifted to Ronnie, whose smooth skin and facial beauty marks were more traditionally appealing.

With a flash of red-painted nails, Ronnie slid him a single sheet. "This is the press release for later today. You're the only one getting it early and Dr. Bingham is here for questions. We're grateful you can work with us on the short delay."

Despite her graciousness with the coffee and donuts, Ronnie's movements were strangely robotic. Atypical of her usual flowing dark locks, the tight bun made her face too pinched for someone not yet thirty. Instead of the usual skirt and sleeveless blouse, her body was encased like a coffin by a dark pantsuit with the shirt collar buttoned tight under her chin. Her eyelids drooped, absent the vivid colors which usually accentuated an extroverted expression.

When Nancy glanced away from the PIO to her lengthy notes, Chuck reviewed the press release. "So he's a young adult from southeastern Arizona with travel from China. How old, what town, and where in China?"

A caffeine boost from a third sip of steaming coffee alerted Nancy to his trap. "Mr. Bresnitz, we're not releasing gender. If the patient was from Phoenix, we'd give more information. In a less-populated area, details compromise privacy."

"So does he have this coronavirus or not? I heard there are others, too."

"Three family members have milder symptoms, plus some hospital staff of concern. But none are currently hospitalized, and all are recovering."

She hesitated with the slight obfuscation. Dr. Carol Russell had been released last night.

His entire body convulsed in a skeptical scoff. "You're amazingly slow to figure out what's going on. You call yourselves medical detectives. Not competent ones, in my book."

Nancy double-downed on cooperation. "We've only been aware of possible Arizona cases for two weeks, and others in the US are also recent. Initial studies found multiple suspect viruses, but the evidence is converging on a coronavirus."

She reached into her folder and pulled out a printout. "*The Lancet* medical journal released an article that should be helpful."

He pointed to the top of the page. "A lot of Chinese names. Am I going to understand this?"

With her pink pen, Nancy circled the Interpretation section. "They isolated a coronavirus from two Chinese patients and used polymerase chain reaction—PCR—for genetic material that matches the virus. They also detected antibodies, which are part of the body's defense system for the virus."

"Are we doing those tests here?"

Ronnie jumped in. "Our state lab is consulting with CDC. We hope for laboratory confirmation within the next week."

"The initial results in China," Nancy added, "indicate this is a new coronavirus, not the same ones associated with the common cold or other outbreaks of pneumonia in military personnel."

Chuck leaned back, chest puffed up. Nancy glanced down to make sure the chair legs stayed on the floor, and he didn't rock back into an embarrassing splat. "I've done medical stories in my time," he said. "Viruses aren't alive 'cause they can't live outside tissue cells. And they require particular species as their hosts."

He knew a lot more than the average reporter. Nancy smiled and shoved the donut box closer to him. "You're talented at this. Viruses tend to be more species-specific than bacteria because the viruses interact with the host animal cells to invade. But when a virus spills over to other species, it can be nasty. Some animals are adapted to living with viral infections—they're called reservoir species. The spillover animals can suffer more clinical damage and death."

Red sprinkles trickled down the front of Chuck's yellow shirt as he chewed between words. "What animals do we got with this?"

"Not my area of expertise and too early to say."

With his last bite, Chuck slipped his pen into his shirt pocket, drawing Nancy's attention to the slight blue stain at the bottom of it. "Thanks for the article," he said. "I'll call you with questions."

Nancy shook his sugar-sticky hand. "Of course. Newspapers do a more thorough job on complex public health issues than television." She smiled, happy she hadn't shared his donut fetish and didn't have to worry about sprinkles in her teeth. With any luck, the compliment would dissuade him from criticizing what they didn't know.

After Ronnie escorted him to the door, Nancy cornered her. "You were unusually quiet, but this is scary, with lots of room for us to look bad. We usually have lab confirmation much quicker."

"You're right, it's a big deal." Ronnie's dark eyes ducked to the floor. "Possibly a new disease—just want to do the right thing."

Nancy sensed she wasn't hearing the full story. "Your daughter Abril, how old is she now?"

Ronnie's eyes sparkled like fireflies. "She's three, the apple of her abuela's eyes. Thank God I have Mamá to do childcare, especially when I'm out-of-town for work." She hesitated, then put a hand on the table. "I'm blessed by her backup with Abril's dad no longer in the picture." She paused again and asked, "Do you ever travel with Dr. Gonzalez?"

Wondering where the conversation was going, Nancy pulled out a chair and offered one to Ronnie. "He usually sends me out on my own except for those border conferences between the US and Mexican states."

Plopping down across from Nancy, Ronnie appeared to measure her words. "At those meetings, how much time do you spend together?"

"Some, I guess." Nancy didn't blush easily, but memories of those exotic gatherings induced a flush through her veins. "My significant other, Fred Grinwold, the New Mexico State Epidemiologist—he's always there too, so my free time is fairly full."

Ronnie licked her fingers and smoothed a few stray hairs back from her forehead toward her bun. "Yeah, I understand." She stood up and headed for the door. "Chuck's unlikely to give us a preview, but I'll email you if he does. Thanks."

Nancy's Spidey powers detected something else going on. Dr. Gonzalez was short-tempered, like Fred. Had Ronnie gotten a dressing down? Being young, she probably wasn't used to rolling with the punches, going along to get along.

Speaking of grouchy men, Nancy needed to call hers and arrange another *American Idol* date. They watched the episodes from their respective state capitals and argued over the contestants. Fred was a fan of Ruben Studdard's smooth rhythm-and-blues stylings, whereas Nancy was a sucker for Kimberley Locke's rendition of Bonnie Raitt's *I Can't Make You Love Me*. Hopefully, no matter when Chuck released his report, she'd be home for dinner and her TV date.

Phoenix, Arizona—Tuesday, April 18, 2003

Ten days after his first article, Chuck called Nancy in her office. "Thanks, Dr. Bingham, for turning me onto the CDC *MMWR*. Today it announces 208 suspected SARS cases from thirty-four states but doesn't list the states. Any additional info you can provide? Some of those new ones from Arizona?"

"Chuck, I don't have more beyond our initial novel coronavirus infection confirmed by CDC. Like some other cases, exposure appears to be Hong Kong. We never got confirmation on family contacts, and everyone's fine now."

His grunt echoed through the receiver. "Did he stay at the Hotel M linked to some of the Hong Kong cases?"

Nancy admired his thoroughness. "We're not releasing that information yet."

"The article mentions spread to healthcare workers. Anyone else at Safford Hospital come down with SARS?"

Almost answering no, she caught his trick. The press release said southeastern Arizona, so his was a reasonable guess. "We're not releasing the hospital name but worked with them to follow the staff. Nothing else was confirmed."

He laughed. "Thanks, Doc. I'll check in with Safford Hospital to see if they want to add something."

She sighed. How to dissuade him without confirming his suspicion? Dr. Oswald was one of the initial suspect cases who never met the case definition, and Nancy still worried about him working overtime at an advanced age. But he told her he lost his wife a decade earlier to colon cancer and the hospital was his family—he wasn't giving it up for anything.

A knock on the door interrupted her ruminations about how to handle Chuck. The door swung open so hard, it banged on the wall. Ronnie's long hair was disheveled, and her cheeks wet with tears.

"Chuck, other things are brewing," Nancy said, "and I've got to go. But call again if I can be of help."

She waved Ronnie in. "What's the matter? Something with your family or the office?"

"I need to put this out within the hour." Ronnie's voice was ragged and soft, unlike the bird-sweet tones of the confident press flack who represented their health department so well. She put the press release on the desk. "Dr. Gonzalez has been fired. And it's all my fault."

Chapter Four

Phoenix, Arizona—Friday, April 18, 2003

Not prone to crying herself, Nancy was uncertain how to interpret Ronnie's tears or the monstrous news about her boss losing his job. Sure, he was an asshole at times, but what could have led to this? And Ronnie said she was responsible.

Nancy helped raise three siblings and knew when to comfort. She pulled the younger woman close, patting her on the back as Ronnie's shuddering sobs shook them both. With a free hand, Nancy groped in her purse for a tissue and pressed it on Ronnie's reddened cheeks, then handed it to her.

"I can't help unless you talk to me." She glanced quickly at the press release Ronnie had delivered. Dr. Gonzalez was resigning as State Epidemiologist at the Governor's request, with the health department's deputy director named as the temporary replacement. But he was an administrator with no epidemiology training.

Ronnie drew back, took a couple of deep gasps, then straightened her blazer. Her words were a whisper. "I shouldn't say any more."

"You started here in health education right out of high school." Nancy hoped that flattery would loosen Ronnie's tongue. "My job hasn't changed, but you've risen to be the Public Information Officer for the whole department, an astonishing achievement. We've worked together almost a decade—you can trust me."

Glancing first to the closed office door, Ronnie nodded and slowly started to speak. "You have a right to know. You're the only other public health physician doing epi, so you might get picked to replace him long-term. He pressured me to join him on a number of out-of-town trips. I thought it might make sense in my PIO role. But away from the office, things got personal."

She paused and Nancy probed. "Can you be more specific?"

"He was careful here, but at night on the road, he'd invite me up to his room after dinner. He knew I was single. I didn't want to cross that line, but he kept at it. Finally he berated me for violating the dress code in the office. I was too provocative, he couldn't concentrate, that kind of thing. When I refused the next trip, he tried to write me up for insubordination."

Nancy shook her head, repulsed by Ronnie's story. "I'm so sorry you went through all that. You should have told me earlier."

"Dr. Gonzalez made the mistake of writing his recent demands in emails. They weren't explicit, but the intent was clear."

"Thank goodness there's a paper trail. So many women aren't believed. I can't imagine you handling press inquiries about his firing—someone like Chuck Bresnitz is sure to ask why he lost his job." Her chest tightened. "I hope Dr. Gonzalez doesn't try to put the blame on you."

The tears started again, and Nancy flinched at her unthinking warning. "Ronnie, I'm sorry, Just trying to anticipate the consequences. This is all too common, I fear. Would you like to go home early? If you want more time off next week, tell me."

Nancy followed through. Ronnie was approved for sick days and Nancy was put in charge of the SARS outbreak.

"Do a good job with this China virus situation," her new acting boss said. "No way I want to keep this extra title long-term. Maybe you'll get appointed as the new State Epidemiologist."

Safford, Arizona—Friday, April 25, 2003

After Dr. Oswald phoned about a new case, Nancy met him in his hospital director office.

"I'm relieved your symptoms last month never were confirmed as SARS," she told him.

"No more than me," he joked. "I thought we were done with it."

Nancy began to take notes. "I wonder if Elijah caught it from his cousin Ammon."

"Elijah was in Toronto."

"That's unfortunate—a Pennsylvania patient was infected by attending a retreat there."

He rested a hand on her shoulder. "The Latter-day Saints are sensitive to this becoming a bigger deal. Thanks for warning me about that reporter."

"I'm a Texas girl, so we're independent and ornery. But it's possible the religious connection might leak out for our patients." She never worked at CDC and didn't have an in with them like Fred. She'd have no control on when they issued an *MMWR* report naming Arizona as a state with multiple cases.

"Glad you're ready and rarin' to go." Dr. Oswald clapped her on the back. "You try to manage those revelations, but first, let's check on our latest patient."

They took an abundance of caution and paused outside the ICU window. Elijah was conscious with an oxygen mask—he waved and smiled. More heavily muscled than his cousin, he must have engaged in heavy work or lifted weights. Maybe his physical fitness kept him from deteriorating to a ventilator.

"Like Ammon," Dr. Oswald said, "Elijah's symptoms were nonspecific. Without respiratory signs or Asian travel, staff didn't initially suspect SARS."

Nancy answered Elijah's wave with a thumbs up. No SARS deaths had been reported from any state and it looked like the trend would continue.

"With severe diarrhea at our ER on Monday, he was given IV fluids and metronidazole, then discharged," Dr. Oswald added. "On Tuesday he returned with shortness of breath and we found bilateral interstitial infiltrates, so admitted him to the ICU. Today his dad mentioned Toronto when I called him about Elijah's antibody results."

"I assume you collected contact information."

Dr. Oswald pulled out a list from the pocket of his white coat.

"Here's four healthcare workers with unprotected exposure before we suspected SARS. I poked my head into his exam room to consult for only a moment."

"Are these staff still working? The N95 respirators I recommended should reduce nosocomial spread."

He nodded. "We're short-staffed—can't afford to have them off work for such a low possibility. With a second SARS case, is there anything else we should do?"

She waved his list. "I appreciate your dilemma with staffing, but these four should stop working for ten days after their contact with him. Monitor temp twice daily; report fever and respiratory signs to your occupational health clinic. Toronto is requiring home isolation and social services brings everything they need to their doorsteps, so they don't go out."

"All right—I'll handle it. Our LDS residents are generous and well-organized."

Nancy handed him back the list and her pen. "Give me Elijah's address and I'll check out the family contacts."

"They're in Thatcher. His dad runs the grocery store there."

"Dr. Oswald, you said your contact with Elijah was limited, but I hope you're taking your temperature, too."

He sighed. "Intermittent cough. Mulberry trees are blooming—it's probably spring allergies."

"You should consider a ten-day furlough."

"Can't remember when I've had that length of time off. I'd go stir crazy. There's a cot in my office, I'll lie down there."

She guided him in that direction. "You do that. I'll check back later today."

Elijah's father held open the store front door for Nancy. He admitted returning a half hour earlier from a visit to his primary-care provider who diagnosed acute viral syndrome and prescribed amoxicillin. At the news, she pulled a mask from her bag and slipped it on, despite the fear it would decrease cooperation. "Mr. Musser, did your doctor inform you that an antibiotic won't help with a virus?"

The man brushed his military-precision haircut, then lifted a can of black beans to the well-balanced pile. "Sure, just covering all the bases."

"Now that your son has been diagnosed with SARS, family contacts should take temperatures twice a day. With your symptoms, I'd prefer you head home and isolate."

He grabbed a flat of condensed milk and began stamping the cans with price stickers. She'd lost his focus—it was vital to tweak his conscience by appealing to the LDS value of community support.

"I'll request the visiting nurse service to stop home and collect specimens for lab testing. You don't want to spread anything foreign to your customers here at the store."

"No backup at the moment. The hospital said there's only a dozen infections in the whole country. I get flu or colds almost every year and you don't make me close the store and stay home."

He had a point. In ten years at the state health department, she couldn't recall requiring full home isolation for disease contacts.

"It's increased to a couple hundred likely cases with forty-five testing positive like your son." She pulled out a second mask. "Please wear this and keep in touch with your primary provider."

At the sound of a grocery cart, he set the mask on the shelf next to the beans and lowered his voice. "All right, doc. I'll put it on when the store is empty. Don't want to freak out the customers."

Without the government regulations and social support systems of Canada, she'd reached an impasse. Family bonds and dedicated health care professionals might be sufficient.

Three hours later, she completed the swing by Elijah's home and his dad's primary care clinic—everyone felt fine. She took temperatures for the relatives and advised them to mention their SARS exposure when seeking treatment for illness.

At a pullout overlooking the Gila River, she hopped out and leaned back on the truck hood. Like a scuba diver ascending to the surface, she sucked in a rejuvenating gasp of spring air. Nothing matched the odors of new life. The soothing sounds of engines from nearby fields and a faint buzz from a bee prompted closing of her eyes as she floated with the joyful sensations. Then the Blackberry chimed—damned technology. It was Fred, and she was grateful for a way to keep in touch.

"Kind of chilly and gloomy, possible snow up in the Santa Fe ski area tonight." His voice was petulant.

Nancy rubbed her bare arms, absorbing vitamin D from the warm Arizona sun. Despite being in adjacent states, they were more than four hundred miles, and four thousand feet of elevation, apart. If he hated the cold so much, why didn't he move to Phoenix?

"Before the storm," he said, "I'm headed over to La Casa Sena for a margarita in the courtyard. Staff are celebrating the retirement of the Chronic Diseases director."

Remembering the verdant patio hidden in the middle of the ancient two-story converted adobe home, a fleeting yearning seeped in for the small-town charm of Santa Fe. But her fond images were from temperate summer visits. In late April, the overhead trellises wouldn't be green. Maybe there'd be crocuses or daffodils.

On too many days, Phoenix traffic and overwhelming heat smothered her like a giant octopus. She rejoiced in her escape as lines of tractors planted cotton seed, rich manure filled her nostrils, and the Gila River tinkled over the gravel bed and boulders.

Repeating her frequent warnings about his diabetes, she ordered, "No salt on the rim of your cocktail glass."

His deep voice growled, a familiar sound to everyone crossing his path. "Yeah, you're not my mother. But you are my lover. How about I drive down early tomorrow? We haven't been birdwatching in a while, and this is prime season for trogon-spotting in the Chiricahua Mountains."

The campground was less than a hundred miles southeast, but duty always came first. "Call me again after your party. We have a second SARS case in the Safford area. Guidelines are stricter and getting contacts isolated is a challenge."

"Thank God we have none in New Mexico yet. I understand if we need to wait another week for our trip. Anytime in May should be good."

"Okay, Fred. Have a good time at your party, and I'll talk to you later tonight."

As soon as she climbed into the truck and turned the key, the Blackberry rang again, followed by the voice of the young nurse from Ammon's room a month earlier.

"Dr. Bingham, I'm calling about Dr. Oswald. He's struggling to breathe and in our second ICU room."

Chapter Five

Safford, Arizona—Tuesday, April 29, 2003

"Is Oswald doing any better?" Fred asked on the morning phone call.

"Not really." Nestled in the motel room's lumpy arm chair, Nancy munched a bagel with strawberry cream cheese, a steaming cup of coffee nearby. She never cried although she'd been bonded with Dr. Oswald like a granddaughter. But the weather manifested her mood. Rainy tears streaked the windows, washing them clean from the ever-present dust. After a lifetime in the desert, rain was her least favorite climate phenomenon. How did people in the Northwest keep from committing suicide?

"He's still unconscious on a ventilator. They considered transferring him to Tucson but this is his hospital. His people want to take care of him."

"Did you see the updated SARS-CoV case definition from CDC?"

"Yes, he's got antibodies plus severe fever and radiographic evidence of pneumonia. He had close contact with a recent SARS patient."

"He also cared for your first case, right?"

Nancy sighed. "Yes, a month ago. Dr. Oswald has been complaining about hay fever since then, so maybe it was a slowly developing infection. Never having a coronavirus like this before, we don't have a clue what it will do next."

"How are you handling everything? You must be short-staffed with your boss getting fired."

"Others are holding down the fort in Phoenix and this is the only SARS cluster in the state. Graham County doesn't have an epidemiologist but their nurse supervisor has been wonderful. I love working with these local health folks—they're incredible representatives of selfless, tireless public service."

"I don't think you'll get hit like Toronto," Fred said. "They've had more than a hundred cases, and WHO declared it the first city outside China to be an international health threat."

He paused and Nancy heard his voice grow faint. "Stephanie, I'll be right with you." Then he came back on the line. "Nancy, you don't sound like your usual gung-ho self. I know the situation with Dr. Oswald is stressful. Any chance you can take a break? You still owe me that birdwatching weekend."

After swigging the rest of her coffee, she lugged the laptop over from the bed with her free hand. "Fred, don't pressure me, you know it doesn't work. If you had cases in New Mexico, you'd be working long hours, too."

"One of the things I love about you—nothing gets you down for long."

"You got that, fella. Hey, if I wind things up early, I'll call you for our *American Idol* TV date. First, I need to talk to a veterinarian. Families are worried about illness and death in their animals. Probably no more than generalized anxiety from a scary, foreign disease."

"Let me know if you need an introduction to Faye Simpson in NYC," Fred said. "Despite my preferring a physician for our next CSTE President, she's sharp. She went through CDC's EIS program like me. Not many vets make the cut for that."

"We're already acquainted, but first I'm going to touch base with our ag department's State Veterinarian. Talk again tonight."

Nancy swore at the forgotten umbrella in Phoenix and left liquid ghost prints on the tile floor as she jogged down the hospital corridor. The young nurse hovered at the ICU suite entrance, clutching the door jamb and sobbing. Nancy's stomach twisted so hard, it felt forced up through her diaphragm. "Dr. Oswald?"

The nurse nodded. "He passed. I . . . was gonna call you . . . just happened." She crunched at the waist and gasped for breath.

As Nancy bent to hold her, she wondered at the girl's extreme reaction. But Dr. Oswald was that kind of guy, worshipped by all the staff members.

"He had a good long life," Nancy said. "He died doing what he loved. This SARS virus is nasty, and we still don't know much about it." She began to shiver as hard as the nurse. "Hun, can you get me a gown? I want to see him."

When the nurse returned, Nancy hugged the fabric tight around her, trying to warm up at the window to the ICU. Staff didn't look in her direction as they unhooked equipment and removed IV lines. Dr. Oswald's face was peaceful, his body at rest, no longer struggling for air. His full shock of thick white hair showed no trace of balding.

Her fingers drifted up to her own, already thinning a few months short of forty. She'd have to check, maybe a side effect of her Chagas parasite infection a decade earlier.

The nurse, tears reduced to soft sniffs, joined her at the window. "He was the one who hired me, fresh out of my LPN program. He liked to give jobs to locals."

"He mentioned his wife dying before him. I'm fuzzy, are there other relatives?"

"A son lives in Marfa, the artist colony."

Only a stone's throw from where Nancy grew up. She'd been so preoccupied with their SARS cases, they never talked about hometowns. She turned away and headed to the human resources office for the son's phone number.

When she reached him on her Blackberry, his sarcasm oozed through the phone. "Hospital said he might not make it. Time catches up with all of us, don't it?"

She gulped. How could a kind, dedicated physician have such

a caustic family relation? "I've never seen a hospital director so involved with his staff and patients."

His bitter laugh was so loud, she held the Blackberry a few inches further from her ear. "Yeah, at the price of his family," he shouted. "Between him and my mother's work as a nurse, my grandmother was the only family member who raised me. And he never spent money on me, just donated everything to international relief charities."

"I'm so sorry," Nancy said. Her own family had branches that never spoke to each other, sawed off, like they never existed. Bonds broken, no forgiveness.

"Mr. Oswald, SARS is a new disease, and an autopsy might be of value. Do we have your authorization?"

"Why the fuck should I care how you handle his carcass?"

Texans talked rough, but this offspring's hatred was new to her optimistic view of life. "Will you want any kind of service or his remains?"

"Dump 'em in the Grand Canyon for all I care."

"All right, we'll arrange everything." She grasped for a thread of connection. "I remember an unusual ceramic piece on his shelf. He bragged about it being made by his son. Assuming that's you, I can assure you he was proud."

The voice on the other end softened to a whisper. "He shoulda done more for his kin."

Nancy verified thorough disinfection of the ICU and a monitoring program for the staff, then refocused on the reports of sick animals. The ag department provided the mobile number for Dr. Ben Smith and said he'd left for Thatcher earlier in the day.

Ribbons of bright sky streaked the horizon as dark clouds lifted. At the wide graveled parking area of the Musser family compound near the river, a man leaned against a Silverado pickup, arms crossed on his broad chest. He reminded Nancy of a football tackle and she thanked heaven she wasn't his opponent. When he tipped his black Stetson, she caught a full view of his bare mahogany head.

He stepped forward to open the door of her F-150 and offer his hand. James Earl Jones issued from his mouth, matching his imposing physique. "Nancy, nice to make your acquaintance. Please call me Ben. I hear you're taking over epi with your boss's resignation."

Once at ground level, she tilted her head up to meet his gaze shadowed by deeply creased eyelids. "With no veterinarian on our side," she said, "I appreciate your expertise." She recalled press criticism of one of his animal disease investigations and could only guess at the stress of his job, keeping everyone happy—the public and animal advocates, politicians and the ag industry. In her own public health career, she rarely faced widespread opposition.

"The Safford hospital director died this morning of SARS," she said. "He's our third confirmed case in the state, and one of the few deaths in the nation. I'm working with our PIO on a release for tomorrow. Attention will be ramped up to a fever pitch. Might have to consider a press conference."

His hand went to his heart. "That's bad news—I feel terrible for his family. My father passed away a few months ago so I know what it feels like."

Nancy swiped at her eyes; death hovered over their meeting. "I'm sorry to hear of your loss. I'm blessed with my family hale and hearty, mostly in southwestern Texas." She considered whether to mention Dr. Oswald's estranged son, then decided against it. "The Mussers called your office about sick animals?"

"Not what I expected from them, you know, self-sufficiency and saving vet costs. But they're blaming animal mortality on this Chinese disease so they figure the government should take care of it. Let's take a quick tour."

He stopped first at a pen with a dozen black-and-white Holsteins, some recumbent in the mud, others chewing on hay. "One death yesterday from calf scours—severe diarrhea caused by environmental problems or multiple microbes. I did a field postmortem and took samples."

Next they strolled down to an area separated from river

bottomlands by barbed wire. With the ground boggy from the early morning downpour, Nancy regretted wearing previously white tennis shoes. The scuffed cowboy boots from her Texas days rested in the corner of her closet floor in Phoenix.

"They graze a few Polled Herefords here for meat." Ben gestured to the stocky brown cattle with pink noses and white hair streaking from their faces down the chest and belly. "A couple calves died with fever and respiratory problems after being moved here from a relative's farm. Shipping fever—multiple viruses and bacteria could be implicated. Vaccines reduce that loss, but they don't believe in them."

At the chicken coop, closer to the house, he pointed to a large rooster with black-and-white spots and a red comb. "Barred Rock, and those hens are Rhode Island Reds, all good for eggs and meat. They lost a few with lethargy and diarrhea, so I grabbed them for testing. Might be bacterial, *Salmonella*."

Nancy scanned her memory for relevant data. "CDC issued a report on human *Salmonella* Enteritidis infections from eggs. A couple thousand hospitalizations and thirty or so deaths."

"The Mussers didn't know washing eggs with cold water can pull in germs, so I suggested rubbing dirt off with a cloth."

A blonde girl with pigtails rounded the chicken coop corner hugging and kissing a small white bird with fluffy plumage. "My family had a backyard flock of Silkies like those," Nancy said. "Keeping kids from doing that will be a challenge."

He nodded. "I'm headed to the next household for follow-up on lamb mortality. If you're checking in with them on human symptoms, I'll leave you to dissuade the kids from chicken love."

"Any info about coronaviruses and domestic animals?" Nancy asked.

"For this new human strain? Not sure when we'll know anything."

"Ben, thanks for the update. With any luck, all this animal morbidity and mortality is unrelated." She breathed in earthy fragrances released by the morning deluge. "I love escaping the city monster, and it's such a blessing that Ammon and Elijah recovered. I wish Dr. Oswald hadn't been collateral damage."

Chapter Six

Phoenix, Arizona—Friday, May 2, 2003

Nancy tightened the chin strap under her lavender sombrero to keep it from flying off in the breeze. In the slanting morning rays, the rocky crag of Squaw Peak alternated charcoal and Saharan puzzle pieces, all tinted with a rosy glow. Although the Phoenix climb was a popular sunset tradition, she liked avoiding crowds. But crashing waves of Ujjayi breaths from the half-dozen yoga enthusiasts drifted over as they practiced sun salutations in the small flat area at the summit.

Piestewa Peak, that's what she should start calling it. Second highest point in the Phoenix Mountains and renamed for Lori Ann Piestewa, killed in April in Iraq. The first known Native American woman to die in combat for the US military, except the peak renaming was controversial and still not official.

Her Blackberry rang and she answered in a whisper. "Faye, thanks for the return call, but I'm disturbing a group imbued with spiritual sustenance. Let me move down the mountain and call you back."

She stepped cautiously on the rough path, careful not to lose her footing or twist an ankle on carved steps or loose rock. Stairway to heaven or hell? Coming down, it was definitely the latter despite the easier breathing. On one steep stretch she grabbed the short line of pipe handrail and paused for a western view of the Valley of the Sun with the White Tank Mountains peeking through streaks of clouds.

At a bench under the limbs of a palo verde, she returned the call from New York City. With few older female colleagues in public health leadership, she respected Dr. Simpson. "I found a spot along the trail where I won't disturb anyone."

"I just realized it's only six-thirty—you Arizona anarchists hate daylight savings time. What are you doing out so early?"

"Best time of day for exercise. I need info on the zoonotic aspects of SARS—we don't have a vet on staff."

"Well," a slurping sound filtered through the phone, "no one's sure about the animal role. But pigs, cattle, chickens, dogs, and cats all get coronaviral infections."

"Yeah, I met with our State Veterinarian on Tuesday. He was checking out illnesses and deaths in the animals associated with our two missionaries."

"We don't know the original animal species but with almost fifty million people dying in the Great Chinese Famine forty years ago, people still rely on live wildlife markets. Some humans working at one in Guangdong have a high rate of SARS antibodies."

As Nancy's body heated in the scant shade, she adjusted position. "What animal species might be implicated?"

"Masked palm civets and raccoon dogs have viruses genetically similar to those in humans. A Chinese ferret badger had antibodies."

"Excuse me, but I never heard of those creatures."

Another slurp came from Faye's end of the call. "Sorry, getting my caffeine fix. Civets are cat-sized mammals that live in trees, raised for fur and food. Raccoon dogs are wild dogs farmed for fur. They look a bit like raccoons but no relation. Chinese ferret badgers are the smallest badgers and associated with rabies outbreaks."

"Do pets have any association with SARS?"

"In one large Hong Kong apartment outbreak, some cats have antibodies. People are freaked and killing cats. Both may have been infected through sewage."

A young couple climbing the trail drew close. "Listen, Faye, my spot here is getting warmer and less private. You're a wealth of good information."

"Happy to help, Nancy. You should be the official State Epi, not just Acting. Women need to be in leadership positions."

"Couldn't agree with you more. I'm not married, no kids, so they won't be worried anything will distract me."

Faye chuckled. "You go, girl. That's the confidence I like to see."

After cleaning up at home and driving to her office, Nancy called Santa Fe.

"Better not cancel the Chiricahuas." Fred's words were a staccato warning.

"No way, but I need to swing by Safford Hospital to verify infection control."

His voice oozed like Texas molasses. "Sweet—you're headed in the right direction. I reserved a Cave Creek Canyon cottage with a kitchenette. Should I pack food in my cooler?"

"Sounds fantastic—surprise me with the menu."

"I'll email you the address and head south around noon. At four hundred miles but interstate most of the way, I should arrive around six."

"Don't hotfoot it and take unnecessary chances. Get your singing voice in good condition on the long drive. You said if I committed to this rendezvous, you'd deliver a Freddie Mercury rendition of *Too Much Love Will Kill You*."

Choking noises were heard through the Blackberry. "If I ever promised that, I must have had way too many margaritas."

Thatcher, Arizona—Friday, May 2, 2003

At the Musser household, everyone was relaxed and healthy. With the temperature in the nineties and Nancy's armpits dark with sweat, Mrs. Musser offered a glass of ice tea. Nancy's luck held at the hospital—no staff out sick. But the black crepe draped over Dr. Oswald's picture crushed her mood. His replacement, Dr. Russell, spoke movingly about the memorial service and mentioned the floral bouquet sent by Oswald's son.

Nancy's funk intensified at missing the service due to the press conference—impossible to cover all the bases when short an epidemiologist. Would they ever name Dr. Gonzalez's replacement if she didn't nag them? She said her goodbyes and rushed back out to the healing power of nature.

Her pickup raced around the eastern slopes of Mount Graham,

also called Dził Nchaa Sí'an, one of the Western Apache's four holiest mountains. Last summer she camped with Fred at Riggs Flat Lake, and they caught their limit of trout within a few hours. No lake or fishing on this trip, but the birdwatching would be a great alternative.

Turning east on I-10, she passed the twin cusps of Dos Cabezas peaks, like little cat ears poking into the crystal blue sky. With every mile of searing sunshine and broad vistas, her mood lifted. At San Simon, she turned onto a two-lane road. Soon the pecan orchards were left behind, replaced at the small village of Portal by a swath of green carpeting the canyon below rocky crags.

The cabin's horizontal wooden planks glowed orange as the sun approached the tips of carved peaks to the west. She settled into an ancient rocking chair on the raised porch, sheltered by a tin roof. Fred drove up in his silver Chevy Impala right on time.

"What are you doing out here?" He pulled her into a tight embrace, out of sync with his grumpy tone. "Did you pick up the keys from the office?"

"Sorry, this setting was too bucolic. Been a while since I could sit in the quiet, Blackberry not working, birds trilling and Cave Creek burbling."

He smiled. "Your life has been more hectic than mine lately. Stay right there while I check in."

"Yeah, starting the day by climbing Piestewa Peak was not the smartest. But facing long hours in the truck, I'd go nuts without my run or hike."

He hugged her again. "Fine with me if you want to keep fit, lean, and mean. More stamina for other things."

Once the cabin was unlocked, she investigated the kitchen drawers and pulled out a pink frilly apron printed with a raccoon in a chef's hat saying **World's Best Cook**. With a grin, she tied it around Fred's thick waist.

Two cans of beef stew simmered in a pot on the electric burners while she made a salad. The sky paled to yellow as the sun dropped behind the canyon walls. She carried the food out to the porch and its wobbly table, then wedged a flat rock under one leg to make it level.

"Things under control in Safford?" he asked, bringing a spoonful of gravy to his lips.

"Yeah, we established quarantine guidelines like Toronto's. The few symptomatic staff were given paid sick leave and separated from family for ten days. We're lucky to have volunteers bringing them everything they need—most communities can't pull that off."

He unscrewed the cap on the Glenfiddich and poured her a dash of whiskey. "Sounds like a Guangdong businessman was the first case in November, followed by a doc in a Hong Kong hotel. Guests spread it here and in Canada."

She grabbed his arm and pointed in excitement to the hummingbird hovering over the feeder hanging from the porch. He opened his bird book and looked it up. "Blue-throated. Must be a male to see that much iridescence at his gorget—his throat."

Salad bowl empty, she pushed it to the center of the table. "SARS globally is about seven thousand cases with over seven hundred deaths. Travel industry's been hit hard with superspreaders in planes and hotels. Not sure how we got so lucky to only have three cases."

"Don't count your chickens. Toronto just reported thirty-three cases related to a close-knit international Catholic sect, exposed at a funeral."

She stood to clear the table. "Thank God we never experienced that. Mind if we turn in early? My muscles are sore from my steep hike this morning. With this quiet, I'll sleep like the dead."

"While I wash dishes, why don't you look in my suitcase? I picked up something you might like."

Inside the main compartment of his bag, the shimmery blue of a floor-length silk gown was easy to spot. When she twirled it through the air, he glanced over his shoulder, hands immersed in soap bubbles. "Two months since we've been together. Can't wait to see how that looks on you."

With one hand, she stroked his broad shoulders. "Let me entertain you." She unbuckled her belt and let her pants drop to the floor. As she struggled with the buttons of her blouse, he joined her next to the bed and caressed her belly. He unhooked her bra, then tugged down her lavender underwear. Wrapping her body in the gown's drapery, she jumped up to stand on the bed and pose like a supermodel.

"You look scrumptious." He dropped his glasses to the shelf built into the wall and when they fell to the floor, didn't pick them up. "Let's see how it feels." He pulled her toward him, their eyes finally at the same level for a gentle kiss. After he lowered her to the white sheets, she kicked a bare leg into the air and stroked her calf.

"Thanks for making this gown long. Too many hours of Texas sun. Skin's not looking as smooth as it used to but I can pretend I'm still in college."

"You're the best-looking almost forty-year-old I've ever seen. I don't want to hear another complaint until you're sixty."

"Well, right now I'm so tired, I could be that old. Get your own clothes off and join me."

Lying in bed, she studied his physique as he obeyed her command. He wasn't conventionally handsome, but then she didn't have to fight off hordes of other women. She smiled to think that no one else ever saw him this way, naked and vulnerable. She liked the firm muscles maintained at the gym, usually hidden under his plaid jackets. It was a kick to boss around a guy who could break her arm like a toothpick, when in reality he was gentle as a lamb.

Her eyes drifted down as he bent to remove his boxers, then closed in sleep.

Portal, Arizona—Saturday, May 3, 2003

The smell of bacon drifted from the Idlewild Campground stirring to life. Nancy and Fred, full up on coffee and cold cereal, trudged rapidly through towering oaks and sycamores along Cave Creek.

She bounced on her toes. "The elegant trogons come back north in the spring. They're so huge, we should find them if we listen carefully."

Faint dog barks drifted down from the canopy. She glanced around and didn't spot any people or pets on the trail. "That could be one. Their caw sounds like a distant dog barking, even when close by," she whispered. She pulled up her binoculars and studied the trees. "We should look for woodpecker holes where the trogons nest."

As Fred juggled binocs and glasses, Nancy spotted it first. "Right there, see the bright red front separated from the green head by the white stripe?"

"He's a monster," Fred smiled. "Built like me."

"As much as I enjoy your nether parts, you don't have that fabulous black-and-white barred tail."

When the trogon flew away, they continued along the trail, searching the treetops. After a fainter, shorter caw, they used the binoculars to spot a female with a gray head and chest. Fred whipped out his life list. "Wow, what a great addition. Not sure why we waited this long to work in this trip."

Trogon hunting was addicting with the sightings so rare, providing intermittent and unpredictable rewards. Nancy's neck and shoulders strained with the constant upward scanning. As the sun reached its apex and pierced the tree cover, her sweating increased and her stomach rolled over.

"Fred, how about we take a rest?"

"Of course. You're a bit pale, working way too many hours with hardly a break since this SARS. Every patient you take to heart, like they were your own kin."

After guiding her down the trail to a picnic table, he pulled a granola bar from his daypack. "You probably need this—we ate breakfast in a hurry to get out here and catch the birds."

Her stomach tweaked again, and she shook her head. "Not yet, just a drink of water."

She let her eyes rest on the alligator-plated bark of the Arizona Madrone draping its lance-shaped leaves over the table with pinkish flowers clustering at the end of reddish stems. With a musical warble and chewee notes, a Painted Redstart flitted between the tree limbs, pausing to show off its bright red breast, white wing patches contrasting its black body.

"Fred, grab your list. Another species with a limited range."

He swiped pine needles from the bench to join her and pulled out his bird guide. "Two new ones by lunch—that's an accomplishment. And you found them before me."

Using both hands, she rubbed her stiff neck and shoulders. After logging the new bird, his strong hands replaced hers. "Is this walk too much? I hoped for a relaxing vacation. They're making you do the work of two people since Gonzalez left."

She brushed his hands aside. He was always criticizing her job in hopes of luring her to New Mexico. She didn't want or need his overprotectiveness, thinking she wasn't smart enough to cope with the increased demands. "They're considering me for the permanent position."

His metal water bottle clunked on the concrete table surface. "How does that solve anything? Will they hire a replacement for you? New Mexico's population is less than a third of Arizona's, so we're okay until I recruit a new assistant."

She challenged him with a smug look. "Why did your last one quit? Drive him away with your demands?"

He grimaced. "He wanted a bigger pond and moved to New York." His fingers grabbed her chin so their brown eyes locked. "I wanted him to leave so you'd join me."

She knocked his hand away again. With a rush of internal heat despite the shaded setting, she didn't want skin contact. "My working for you would kill our relationship. Some could negotiate the boundaries, but not us. I got used to Dr. Gonzalez telling me what to do, not you."

The twinge in her stomach spread upward to her throat. Heartburn. She didn't usually have cold cereal—maybe lactose intolerance.

"You don't think a woman is cut out to be State Epi." Picking a fight increased the sensation of a tight chest. He'd never criticized her ambition, but his sniping at the Glenwood Catwalk about Faye

Simpson becoming CSTE President made her wonder. What was his problem with Faye, her being a woman or being a veterinarian?

"I'm just a guy who wants to marry his girl and start a family. Your biological clock doesn't give us any time."

She tugged the tails of her chambray shirt out of her jeans to filter cool air. "I'm about to achieve my lifelong dream, and you bring this up now." Her fist pressed against her breastbone.

His fingers went to her wrist. "Nan, you're not looking very good. Pulse is surprisingly rapid considering we're only sitting."

"You just pissed me off." She stood up and tried to pull her legs out from under the table, then sank back down and lowered her head to Fred's lap. The difficulty in catching her breath worsened. "I'm not feeling well. Doc ten years ago mentioned possible heart problems after my Chagas infection."

"Don't remind me. I've worried ever since. Are you having chest or arm pain?"

"More like you're grabbing my chest with your hammy fist."

"Considering that my hand's not on your torso, that's alarming." He pulled out his Blackberry. "I'm not getting a phone signal. Let me see yours." After rummaging for it in her pack, he set it on the table. "Dammit, no connection. They might have cell service and an EMT in Portal."

"Can you sing Freddie Mercury 'til we get there?" She welcomed his arm wrapped under her shoulder with hand tight to her rib cage, almost carrying her to the next campsite. A young couple eating sandwiches looked up as they approached.

"Buddy," Fred asked, "you need to run us into town. I'm a doctor, and we've got a medical emergency."

Sleeping Coronaviruses

By early January, 2004 when the US government bans civets from importation, the SARS virus in humans vanishes, its impact primarily on Asia.

Despite its mysterious absence for almost a decade, the US in 2012 declares SARS-coronavirus a select agent with potential to pose a severe threat to public health and safety.

Firenze

This story is modified from an earlier version released by "Mystery Tribune" and features characters from the novels.

Óscar dropped the two-foot long fiery red dragon next to Janey on the bedspread and it crept closer to her. She screamed and leapt up behind him, almost knocking him over. He didn't anticipate hysterics—she was a matter-of-fact scientist.

"What the fuck is that?" Her voice was low and angry. "And why in hell would you put it on the bed with me?"

"We both love animals—I've cuddled all three of your cats and your dog."

Tawny hair lashed tanned shoulders as she shook her head in a rage. "We've been dating almost six months and you never mentioned a plan for *this*."

"Lo siento." He beamed a Poe Dameron grin—it always paid off before. His fingers stroked her bare arms exposed by the sleeveless lime-green sundress she had worn to the August barbecue and pool party. Her muscle relaxation, the leaning into his body—that was predictable. The power of their sexual chemistry was undeniable. Until Firenze hissed.

The beardie pumped its long body up and down like a weightlifter. Its scaly head bobbed, one clawed hand traced circles in the air, and its throat pouch ballooned a haunting black. The jaw gaped, stretching with each sound, flashing dozens of small sharp teeth.

As Janey scooted toward the bedroom door, he steered her to the leather recliner where she perched, ready to escape.

When he reached over to stroke the lizard's long banded tail, its mouth closed. With care, he draped it around his neck. "Incredible, isn't he?"

"Yeah, right," she answered. "You still haven't said where it came from. Or what it is."

After he cranked his neck to give it a kiss, she grimaced and wiped the back of her hand over her lips.

"He's a bearded dragon—originally from Australia. All different sizes and colors, but Firenze is an adult, full-grown."

He was familiar with the no-nonsense epidemiologist look that came over her square face. Brown eyes flashed under long dark lashes. "Is he legal?"

Not a surprise she would ask that, but he had no idea. "I bought Firenze from a guy over in Deming who I met at my restaurant. Beardies live a couple of decades. This handsome fellow was more work than the guy anticipated."

The dragon squirmed and Óscar used both hands to stabilize it. "I could never have a dog or cat like you. With my restaurant, I'm never home. But when I am, I'll no longer be alone. It's comforting to hear him shifting around in the enclosure when I fall asleep."

Her skepticism still clear, Óscar lowered the animal back into the glass container in the front corner of the walk-in closet. "He's not that aggressive most of the time—he doesn't know you yet."

"When did you move all this in? I was only in Phoenix for a week at the immunization conference." She stood at the door, waving her arm past Firenze's house to take in the mini-frig and rubberized containers. "Do you think this is a romantic atmosphere?"

He flushed—she was right. He needed to make amends.

"I'm sorry to startle you. We'll close the closet door when you sleep over. I couldn't let Firenze get dumped in the desert. He wouldn't know how to fend for himself."

Óscar dangled collard greens toward her and attempted a kiss, but she blocked his lips. As her fingers accepted the veggies, he guided her arm toward the open tank top. "Feed him one leaf at a time—he loves it. I promise he won't bite."

While she was distracted, he pulled out his insect containers and a white plastic bowl, sprinkling calcium powder along the bottom. Small gray crickets danced inside, trying to escape as he coated them with the bone-strengthening mineral. Next he dumped wriggling brown meal worms and yellowish wax worms into the mix, still stirring. He handed her the bowl.

"Will these little guys freak you?"

She shrugged. "I'm okay when they're contained like this. But they look uncomfortably similar to bot fly larvae that crawl into our open wounds or bury under our skin, later breaking out."

He twitched. "And you think Firenze is ferocious? You public health people have gross stories."

After coating small Dubia roaches and a few three-inch Madagascar hissing cockroaches with the powder, he handed one of the larger ones to Firenze with a pair of tongs. The long pink tongue flashed forward as Firenze gulped the bug.

She flinched. "Roaches? As if Tucson apartments aren't already plagued enough by them."

He placed the glass lid on the aquarium and changed the subject. "Bet you're wondering how he got his name."

"Not really, but I'm sure you'll tell me."

"Ezio Auditore da Firenze is an Italian nobleman and master assassin in *Assassin's Creed*."

He dangled bok choy to Firenze's flitting tongue and she headed to the bathroom. "I didn't realize you were one of those video game nerds," she shouted over the sound of running water.

Coming up behind, he pressed himself against her bright short skirt. "I was into it more when I was younger. But now, between you and the business, I've no time for teen boy hobbies." He reached around and cupped her breasts. "You're worth it."

She slid out from his embrace and thrust his hands under the faucet. "No touching until you're cleaned up."

Her being forceful, and the finger massage, was a turn-on. Until she added, "And if you want me in your bed, the assassin needs to say adiós."

In early January, Janey's impression when she first met Óscar Hernández wasn't favorable. She offered a firm, confident handshake as she entered Loroco, his high-end Salvadoran restaurant named for an imported flowering vine used in pupusas, the most popular dish. After a New Year's Eve party, more than two dozen patrons had developed projectile vomiting and unrelenting diarrhea.

"For the people at your party," she said, "the state lab confirmed norovirus infection. That's the one you hear about on cruise ships."

"¡Púchica! Sorry, government regulation is all too much. So they spread it among themselves—not my fault."

"You're correct, norovirus can be person-to-person among those sharing ship cabins. In that case, you'll see more prolonged transmission. But these people got sick all at the same time, early New Year's Day, except for a few family members who didn't attend the party and got sick a day later—we call it secondary transmission."

Noticing his dark scowl, she paused, then took a deep breath to finish. "The initial outbreak was point source, same time and place, and the only thing in common is your party."

He stood up and slammed a menu against his desk. "No evidence, just guesswork. My staff are the best—there's no way they did this."

So they didn't meet cute. But she turned on her earnest, low-key charm. She was a researcher, not regulatory like one of the Pima County inspectors—just wanted to solve the mystery and prevent it from happening again. Although he balked, she walked out with the full reservation list and patron phone numbers.

She worked day and night on phone interviews, reaching almost all those at the restaurant on New Year's Eve. Then her statistical analyses comparing those who got sick with those who stayed healthy revealed a strong association with baleada, a Honduran dish. Within a few hours of providing Óscar the results, he asked her to join him during staff interviews.

"Soy tan malo, doctora," a twenty-something line cook said in tears.

"Not a doctor, only a master's degree," Janey answered. The

noisy sobs of the young man were unnerving. In her experience, people didn't admit when they did something wrong. "What happened?"

The cook darted quick glances to his boss, older by a decade. Perhaps it was a bad idea to allow the owner to stay during the interviews. But he insisted, and his charm was irresistible. His posture implied he was used to getting what he wanted. She twisted in her chair as the baleada-maker struggled for words.

Óscar touched her arm. "Señorita Johnson, could I translate? Guillermo is from my hometown of Ciudad Barrios, but he's a recent immigrant. Unlike me, who escaped as a child, he doesn't know English well."

Janey recalled some Spanish from her Tucson High School and U of A classes, but couldn't follow everything that Guillermo said. She picked up Archbishop Romero's name, but looked into Óscar's dark eyes for assistance.

"Guillermo says he wants to be honest and courageous like His Eminence, who was executed during a sermon asking the military to stop repression of the poor."

Fidgeting again, she tapped the pen on her notebook. She appreciated the history lesson but didn't understand its relevance.

"Guillermo's job was stuffing flour tortillas with beans and cheese. He got a rip in his glove but was in a hurry and didn't change it. And he was ill a few days earlier."

Tears continued to leak down the cook's cheeks.

"He feels terrible that he made all those people sick and wants to make penance." Óscar added, "And I take personal responsibility—I shouldn't have dismissed your initial inquiry."

She was impressed that Óscar didn't fire the cook, in light of the black mark on the restaurant's reputation. Instead, he invited her to reinforce food safety protocols for all staff. Although he was intimidating when they first met, during the training she saw the easy camaraderie and professionalism between the boss and his employees.

For her 31st birthday, he phoned her to dine at Loroco.

"I don't have a birthday this year," she protested.

"Your colleague told me, but surely your family celebrates it on February 28 when it's not a leap year."

The skin on her forearms reddened. Thank goodness they weren't on FaceTime where he could see it. "I'm not sure it's appropriate for us to meet socially."

"Okay, I understand you won't accept a meal at my restaurant. But if you can't be friends with people you meet through work, your world will be a lonely place. It's too full of germs—you'll eventually bust everyone in Tucson for their lack of hygiene."

Although his voice was persuasive, she didn't change her mind. Too much overlap with work. But another idea flashed and she made the offer before thinking. "I'm taking the day to explore the Desert Museum. Want to come along?"

An hour later, she waited under a palo verde, bark and branches still olive green even in winter with dropped leaves. As he roared up to the museum entrance on a Harley, she strolled over to greet him.

"Downright balmy." He unzipped the black leather jacket. "My friends in Oracle had snow yesterday."

Not a date. But he was so exotic, like a panther hiding its spots. Too good to be true, especially when the ticket clerk recognized him and summoned the Museum Director.

"Thanks for your generous food donation during our last fundraiser, Señor Hernández." The Director shook his hand. "Would you like a backstage tour?"

If Óscar said yes, she wouldn't have to be alone with him. Why was that a worry when she initiated the invitation?

But he shook his head. "We'll stroll on our own. Pretty quiet today."

"Yes, the bad weather scared everyone off. You might have a few areas to yourself."

They started in Cat Canyon. Somewhere between the bobcats and the ocelot, he held her hand. Somewhere along the Desert Loop trail amid the towering green columns of saguaros, his leathered arm reached down to hug her shoulder.

Electric tingles, despite the clothing separation. She shook her arms to interrupt the confusing sensation. So many months since a date or flirtation—a woman who collected poop samples didn't appeal to most guys.

Behind the wire fence, several javelina rooted in the dirt, while others stretched out, basking in the winter sun. Óscar gestured to the wild boars with coarse salt-and-pepper hair.

"Buddies and I almost got nailed by these guys when camping in the Chiricahuas."

The air cooled and cumulus clouds built up, threatening rain. Like most natives, she loved the smell of the desert in a rainstorm, but shivered. He tightened his embrace.

"They can be aggressive," she said. "I heard of a wildlife park volunteer who got nailed—he wasn't sure which animal. Regulations require euthanasia and testing for rabies."

As he tilted her face up, her heart skipped a few beats. His fingers were warm and roaming, brushing her lips. But the mood was interrupted by his response. "They didn't kill and test them all because of one guy's stupidity?"

"No, no." She pulled away to start down the dirt trail, then turned back to smile and reassure him. "The guy volunteered for rabies treatment, so examining javelina brains wasn't necessary."

"That's a relief," he said. "Animals shouldn't suffer when we're the idiots."

As they exited the grounds at closing time, he tugged her toward the motorcycle. "I have an extra helmet—join me on a ride up Gates Pass for sunset."

Her practical mind went into calculation mode. "Doesn't make sense. We'd have to backtrack here afterward to retrieve my car."

His fingers raked her hair—tiny flashes of lightning at the roots.

"Come on, live dangerously and try something new. Have you ever been on one of these?"

"Why not?" She grabbed the extra helmet, unwilling to admit she'd never ridden a motorcycle. Too many injuries and death in the county health data, although she was capable of leaving those theoretical threats behind. The museum director's respect and the restaurant staff's adoration inspired trust.

After hopping up behind him on the hog, she glued her arms to his sides and slipped her fingers beneath the front of his jacket to press into his belly. With each tilt of the machine through the switchback mountain passes, her fingers slid between the shirt buttons and glued to his hard abdominals. Finally parked at the pass, he lifted her off the bike and kissed her fingers.

"Bit nervous? I might have bruises." His tone chastised but his eyes were friendly. She ducked her own. The ride had been intoxicating, in more ways than one.

On the midweek winter evening, there were few cars in the parking lot. Óscar led her up the steep dirt path higher on the mountain for a private rock perch overlooking the clouds darkening with bright colors.

First came his lips caressing the back of her neck, but she didn't discourage him. Her eyes stayed focused on the western hues, and her skin burned. When he twisted her in his arms so their foreheads touched, she stopped him.

"What are we doing? I'm not anything special."

Both of his hands held her face. "Not special? You must be kidding. Brilliant mind, forgiving heart." He smiled. "And you didn't close me down."

Uncomfortable with the connection between work and personal, she bent away.

"Just kidding." After pulling her back against his chest, hands crept up her torso over the jacket. "Forgot to mention—I'm intrigued with your curves. But with these winter clothes, some of that is supposition."

Had to take a leap sometime—she pulled down her zipper and guided his hand in. "Let's make it more than a supposition."

Dr. Fred Grinwold, New Mexico Department of Health State Epidemiologist, looked up to greet his young mentee.

"Those three siblings in Las Cruces," Maya said, "the ones

hospitalized with *Salmonella* and bloody diarrhea. They all had two different strains, Cotham and Kisarawe."

While swiveling side-to-side on the old-fashioned rocking chair, he tried to remember the first *Salmonella* outbreak during his own two-year Centers for Disease Control and Prevention assignment to the state. Almost a hundred cases had resulted from eating beef jerky. The homemade version was popular yet risky if not processed at sufficiently high drying temperatures and low water activity. But one of the current salmonellosis cases from the southern part of the state was only an infant—unlikely to be chewing on dried meat.

After rubbing his forehead to organize his thoughts, he adjusted his glasses and studied Maya. He wanted a CDC Epidemic Intelligence Service Officer who was a preventive medicine physician like himself. Everyone was more comfortable with a known quantity. But her broad skills as a veterinary epidemiologist had paid off with the anthrax and other outbreaks this past year.

"Friday before Labor Day weekend—why do notifications of outbreaks always come in on Fridays?" He smirked at his own rhetorical question, knowing the answer: concerned patients contacting the doctor's office before closing, the lab finishing its backlog for a lighter load of emergency specimens on Saturday, and the upcoming three-day holiday weekend that amplified everyone's sense of urgency. Only public information officers liked Friday afternoons—a convenient time to release news and avoid subsequent hysteria, with reporters also preferring time off.

"Get down to Cruces and figure out what's going on," he ordered. "About ten percent of *Salmonella* cases are from animal contact, so you're the right person to work with the local office."

After she left, he lifted his shirt and pressed the receiver against the continuous glucose monitoring sensor embedded under the skin. Level fine he didn't want diabetes to interfere with his romantic weekend. He poked **Bingham Nancy** on his contact list and listened for the ring.

She didn't pick up—just a recorded message with her intelligent, aging voice which he still loved after all these years. Whenever they missed connections, he worried about her mild heart attack more than a decade earlier, probably related to the Chagas Disease she contracted from a triatomine bug bite during a 1993 night of passion in Sonora, Mexico. He still blamed himself—if he hadn't slept so soundly, he might have noticed the bug before it exposed her.

"Nan, I'm headed out to Pinetop. I'll meet you at the resort. Still not sure I want to lose money at the casino, but you could always persuade me to do anything."

Nancy awoke to joyful bird song. In the cooler eastern Arizona high altitude, she and Fred had left the window ajar. She opened her eyes to delicate lace curtains filtering soft morning light peeking through the thick ponderosa forest. As she sat up, she clutched the fluffy pink robe around her shoulders.

Some things never changed, even after more than thirty years. Fred snored on the other side of the bed, blissfully unaware of the magical sunrise. She could wake him up, but last night had been rather vigorous.

While she relaxed under the soothing warmth of the shower spray, the frosted door squeaked open and Fred joined her. The stall wasn't large but Fred was, so she couldn't avoid skin to skin contact, even if she wanted to, which she definitely didn't. His thick fingers shoved the hair out of her eyes, then he kissed them. Maybe this never got old because she lived in a separate state and didn't formalize their relationship—was that the secret to long-lasting love? Always wanting more.

After helping him soap up and rinse, she left him alone in the small bathroom to dry off. Dressed in navy pants with a pink sweater over her yellow blouse, she sat on the edge of the bed to yank sensible black tennis shoes onto swelling feet.

He rejoined her in the bedroom, then pulled on his own dark brown pants and shirt. They held hands as they ambled down the corridor to the restaurant.

No sooner had they ordered blueberry pancakes and drinks—

green tea for her, black coffee for him—than her cell phone rang. It was Janey Johnson, the epidemiologist with Pima County.

"Dr. Bingham, sorry to call so early on the holiday weekend. I hope I didn't wake you?" The young woman's voice was courteous, but she sounded stressed.

"I've always been an early riser," Nancy said. "What's up?"

"My boyfriend is hospitalized at Tucson Medical Center with *Salmonella*—two unusual serotypes."

Nancy nodded her thanks to the server who topped off the hot water. She caught Fred's frown. With both being the epidemiologic leaders for their states, they knew it was a 24/7 kind of job. But they got so little time together, with her in Phoenix and him in Santa Fe, he was jealous of any distractions.

She mouthed, *I'm sorry,* and returned to the call. "How's he doing, Janey?"

"Dehydrated—they're giving fluids. Bloody diarrhea, weak. He's the owner of a popular restaurant and works long hours. He doesn't cook, just manages everything."

Nancy stepped through to the outside deck as the server delivered their breakfast and Fred's cell also rang. She settled down on the wooden picnic table after verifying no one else nearby.

"If he was working during his illness," Nancy said with an authoritative tone, "make sure you or the restaurant inspector are reviewing their procedures and doing surveillance for more cases."

She heard exasperation in the young county staffer's voice.

"You don't need to remind me—I'll take care of it as soon as we hang up."

Normally, Janey was the picture of cheerful politeness, but her boyfriend's illness clearly had her rattled.

Fred came into view, holding his cell to his ear while directing the server with hand gestures to move their breakfast outside. Then he sat at the opposite corner of the table, his voice quiet enough to avoid distraction.

"What were those serotypes?" Nancy directed the question into her own iPhone.

"Kisarawe and Cotham," Janey said. "Hope I'm pronouncing the first one right."

"Not triggering my brain cells. I'll call our lab director and see if someone can check for other cases. I can't promise how quickly they'll get that done on the weekend. The earlier noncomputerized records will have to wait until Tuesday."

"Thanks, Dr. Bingham."

"No problem. Let me know if anything changes. I'll be in touch if I hear about more cases from anywhere in the state."

Her index finger detected medium warm pancakes and she took a bite. The call to the state lab could be postponed until after breakfast. Fred continued his conversation while she emptied her plate.

The soft piquant berries burst in her mouth—it must be something urgent if he was ignoring his favorite treat. She dipped a spoon into the whipped cream on top of his stack. She never ordered any, watching her weight, which slowly crept up over time. But stealing some of his frothy topping—not a major dietary sin.

Then she remembered her promise to Janey—phone the state lab. Her mind was slipping lately—shouldn't be feeling old at fifty-six. Recuperation was challenging after the heart attack from Chagas infection, and the doctor had warned her about neuro impacts, too. But mental slowing with age was normal—nothing but low oxygen from high altitude at their ridgetop retreat. Fred's red blood cells were adapted from life in the Sangre de Cristo Mountains of Santa Fe, but hers from living in Phoenix weren't.

By the time she verified no additional cases and no prior record of those serotypes, Fred wolfed down his own breakfast. "They could reheat those pancakes," she said.

"Not worth the wait," he answered, but he waved down the server for more hot coffee.

"You were on a long time," she observed.

He nodded while putting his fork on his plate. "Yes, Maya is in Cruces for a *Salmonella* outbreak. A one-year-old died of bacteremia, and two siblings are hospitalized. Despite antibiotics increasing adverse effects and prolonged shedding, they decided to add them to the treatment protocol for the other kids. They're not recovering and have been hospitalized for a week."

"Interesting." Nancy wiped her syrup-sticky fingers on the cloth napkin. "My call was from Janey Johnson at the Pima County Health Department. Her boyfriend's also very ill with *Salmonella*. What's the chance that cases almost three hundred miles apart are related?"

Several Mountain Chickadees swooped in to battle over the pancake crumbs on the rough-hewn deck, alternating clear trills with more threatening screeches. Birdwatching was one of her favorite, if infrequent, outdoor activities with Fred. But she needed to stay focused on work, sometimes a challenge since the heart attack.

"Cotham and Kisarawe serotypes with matching PFGE patterns for all six of our cases," she dimly heard him say as she pulled her gaze away from the black-and-white-capped birds.

"Could you repeat that?" She shifted closer.

"Not going deaf, are you?" he teased. "I hope you're following up for your Chagas. You remember the doc said you could have effects decades later."

"Fred, you're sweet to worry, but I'm fine. The Tucson case is unusual, two serotypes in the same patient. Arizona hasn't diagnosed them before—Kisarawe and Cotham."

His face flushed—his emotions were always obvious to her. "Same with us. Those strains have been isolated by the National Veterinary Services lab in recent years from bearded dragons."

"What the heck is that?"

He answered with a quick search on his cell phone, and held up a photo. "They're a trending reptile pet. Maya said there's more than fifty million reptiles imported each year, and all are at risk for shedding *Salmonella*."

Nancy shook her head in disgust. "Learn something new every day in public health, often bad. I wonder if it's a *Game of Thrones* effect—you know, the dragons?"

Fred nudged his plate aside and unwrapped his bulk from the bench, then they both stepped around to the end of the table.

"I guess we have work to do." She smiled to soften the blow. "Our horseback ride will have to wait."

"The family with the three infected toddlers has a dragon, and Maya is checking for the other cases. I need to review her draft Epi-X notification to other states." He returned her smile and reached out to ruffle her short gray-salted brown hair. "At least Arizona is already in the loop."

Óscar's brain slowly reawakened, and unfamiliar words filtered in through a long tunnel.

"This is incredibly rare. Most cases of *Salmonella* brain and spinal cord infection—meningitis—occur in children under two years of age. Unfortunately, the mortality rate can be high."

It sounded like one of those high-handed physicians. With a healthy diet, lots of pumping iron and running, he never needed one before.

Then a familiar voice, higher pitched than he remembered—Janey. "Those muscle twitches in his arm, are they like seizures?"

"Yes," the invisible doctor answered. "But we've switched Óscar's antibiotic to a fluoroquinolone. That should be more effective."

As he forced his eyelids open, the room spun in a gauzy haze. He felt hands on his arm tighten and swiveled his head to glimpse her.

"Change in treatment seems to be working. Miss Johnson, can you step back? I need to do a neuro exam."

The next week in the hospital was long and tedious. He couldn't remember ever being flat on his back and mentally sluggish for such a period before. His executive chef stopped by to update him on Loroco. Everything was humming, and no staffer, patron, or friend caught the bacteria from him.

The restaurant completed a deep cleaning, and Janey assisted with environmental sampling. Everything was handled—he could set aside micromanaging for once. Janey assured him she took care of his apartment.

On Saturday, she introduced him to the doc in Phoenix she reported to, Dr. Nancy Bingham. But Janey worked for the county, not the state, so he didn't understand their relationship. The lady was stocky with graying hair and lively brown eyes behind the thick glasses.

Janey and Dr. Bingham huddled in the corner with the neurologist, then Janey floated back to his side. Those lips that he loved to kiss were spread wide as she giggled. What would make her so light-hearted?

"Sweetheart, you're finally testing negative for *Salmonella*. We can go home." Janey never used terms of endearment—clearly the hospitalization had changed a lot of things.

"Mr. Hernández, or can I call you Óscar?"

He nodded, noting Dr. Bingham's maternal arm around Janey's shoulder.

"I don't want to intrude on your homecoming but Janey's one of our best county staff. This week's been rough for her, so I came down to touch base and give her support."

Óscar hated Dr. Bingham pushing his wheelchair to the entrance while Janey pulled her Honda up to the curb, but weakened limbs reinforced cooperation. Janey swung her shoulder under his and helped him into her passenger seat.

"I'll meet you two at the apartment," the lady doc said. Which one, his or Janey's? But when he spotted the stuccoed building, he knew he was home. As Janey jumped out to open his door, the doc met them at the curbside with the lightweight wheelchair. "This fit better in my Odyssey than Janey's Civic."

Janey was chipper as she maneuvered him past the beckoning blue pool. She must have noted his yearning gaze. "Neurologist said swimming will be great therapy—get your muscles in shape again after the bedrest. Tomorrow morning before the temp breaks a hundred?"

He was glad he'd chosen a ground-level place—made it easier for Janey to maneuver inside his front door. The drapes on the sliding glass door to his back patio were wide open. Waving a weak arm in that direction, he asked her, "Could we sit outside for a bit? I miss the sun and fresh air."

After snagging his cowboy hat from the end table, Janey guided him through the door that Dr. Bingham held open and then slid closed.

"Over there in the corner near the rose bush," he instructed. "I want to feel the full force baking my body, and Peace blossom scent for aromatherapy."

"You don't mind if I corner your girl here under the awning?" Dr. Bingham asked. "Direct sun can get too much for me."

He shook his head and rested his eyes, letting his mind and body fully relax. It was wonderful to be home, not a single worry. Life-threatening illnesses had one benefit—a reminder of those he valued most.

Janey's voice drifted in and out.

"Real wakeup call"—good, she was also appreciating the relationship more.

"But he's not so sympathetic to undocumented immigrants"—hell yeah, the Hernández family followed the rules, and others should too.

"He sneers when he talks about Bernie Sanders and socialism"—growing up in an unstable region with fanatics as leaders will do that to you.

"And he's pro-life"—what else would you expect from a good Catholic?

Getting picked on, he wanted to defend himself, but the sun seeping through blue jeans was too enervating. His head dropped to his shoulder—not dozing, but blissful.

Dr. Bingham's voice was more forceful. "Do you want to dismiss half the population who have more conservative views than yours?"

Janey didn't answer.

"Is he generous and kind to his staff and friends? Does he respect you as a career woman?"

Janey's lovely lilt answered that one. "I think so. He's a pain in the butt sometimes, but yes. His parents named him after Archbishop Romero from his home town, who's now a saint. Not a bad role model."

"Respect is paramount—more important than any different beliefs. Sometimes differences enrich a relationship. I never married, but have some experience with that." The older woman's voice halted—was Janey going to respond? He was curious about her answer.

Dr. Bingham continued, "Did you resolve the dragon?"

Firenze—his pet had slipped his muddled mind. One of them had set ice tea next to his chair and he reached for the cool glass. A hit of caffeine should get him back in the ballgame.

"My baby," he said, and their heads both snapped toward him. "Janey, did you take care of him?"

She stood and dragged her lawn chair over. "Of course, Óscar. I gave him all the healthiest foods, like you showed me. But a vet took him for sampling, to find out if he had the same bacterial strain as you. I'm sorry, we have a big outbreak, with many people sick across multiple states. One little girl even died."

His face contorted in horror. They TOOK him?

Janey rushed on. "A group's been smuggling beardies in through Miami. The animal *Salmonella* genetic patterns matched the human cases, including yours."

Dr. Bingham interrupted. "There's no way to clear *Salmonella* from a reptile, and antibiotics haven't been entirely successful with small turtles. These particular strains are very nasty, leading to invasive disease and a disseminated blood infection in the child, neurologic infection for you, and a dozen other serious gastrointestinal cases, including secondary spread within families."

He opened his mouth to argue, but Dr. Bingham held up a hand and continued. "You know the importance of food safety. One New Mexico foodhandler is ill. My counterpart, Dr. Grinwold, and his staff are tracking down restaurant patrons."

With the two women finally in a pause, he straightened his spine and knocked aside Janey's comforting hand. "You KILLED him?"

Janey's hand went back to his shoulder and he let it stay. "Oh, gosh no, Óscar. I'm sorry I couldn't consult with you, but you were unconscious. After Firenze tested positive, he couldn't come back here. Well, they might have allowed it, but I love you and couldn't chance another infection, of you or me."

That expression of love was a new one. Over the past six months, they'd become close, spending as much time together as their busy work schedules allowed. Until Firenze, she practically lived at his place on the weekends. But they both did things related to Firenze without telling the other. That dragon really cast a spell.

"So if he's not dead, where the hell is he?" After her passionate reveal, he regretted the question sounding harsh.

The softness of fingers stroking his brow was soothing, almost enough to settle him down.

"A new reptile museum in Wilcox was eager to give him a home, despite the *Salmonella*. He's a wonderful specimen, and they know how to be careful. Maybe they can do some antibiotic therapy research. So he's not far away. Depending on how your recovery goes, we could visit him next week."

With her eager expression, how could he say no? He wanted to be royally pissed, but her warm eyes were too inviting. Taking both of her hands, he growled in frustration. "Better be thinking of ways to make this up to me."

She was a serious person and he didn't see her grin often. But this time, it was miraculous when she leaned in for a deep kiss, tongue stroking his. Nothing stood in their way.

"Ahem, I should head to Phoenix." The comment from the sidelines reminded him of their audience.

"Excuse me, amante, I'll be right back." So she could use Spanish when trying to get on his good side.

By Thursday, he recovered enough for the eighty-mile trip as a passenger. He never before let anyone drive his gleaming black Lincoln Navigator. But Janey took time off work and spent every minute of the past few days making him feel heavenly. Bubbly cuddles in the bathtub before he felt strong enough to stand in the shower. Lots of whispers of amor, and physical demonstrations of it. A guy should almost croak more often.

His heart rate increased as they hopped out in front of the small adobe walls lining a graveled patio. "Miniature Desert Museum," he said. "Like our first date on your birthday."

He couldn't wait to see his beloved pet again, the only one he ever had. His parents had been strict—money was too tight to waste on animals. As he crawled his way up through the restaurant industry, he'd been too busy to make the commitment to any companion.

Firenze lived with him only a couple of weeks after the purchase, before he got infected. But the dragon had enjoyed the close contact. Perhaps it was in response to the hand that provided food. The hostile encounter with Janey on the bed had been a surprise—she was shorter and presented less of a threatening appearance.

After swinging through the small museum's carved pine doors, he spotted Firenze, front and center in a huge enclosure, uncovered and filled with native plants. His hand snaked out to toss a pelleted treat. There was a double barrier, so he couldn't reach him, but he hoped Firenze would remember the gesture. Until his buddy rose up on all four legs and hissed, tail slashing, and baring those fifty-odd teeth. Traitor. Oh well, time to move onto something softer in bed.

After tugging Janey to a small chortling waterfall in a fake rainforest, he feathered loose brown hair away from her face and pulled her close for a kiss. "How about we formalize this new family, you and me, no bearded lizards?"

He wrested out of his front pocket the family heirloom, then opened his palm to display a sea-blue ring, surrounded with sparkling diamonds. Larimar, one of the rarest gems in the world, found only in one square kilometer of the Dominican Republic. Called the Atlantis stone, with healing properties—just what they needed to stitch together their souls despite all their differences.

What's Within

This story is modified from initial release in "Fiction on the Web" on 5/31/21. It is a MayaVerse prequel at the beginning of the public health career for Faye Simpson, an important mentor to Maya Maguire in the alphabetical novels.

November 11, 1984

The brain cyst glows on the radiologic film hanging from metal clips over the light box. No one, even without medical training, can miss that foreign aberration, an invasion. Like an ostrich egg—fleshy insides encapsulated by a shell. My skin prickles—everything within the sterile room is clammy, including your fingers, cradled in my bare right hand.

Holding the discarded plastic glove in my left, I glance back to the ICU window—no one catches me breaking personal protection procedure. They require a full mask, gown, and gloves after finding the three-centimeter purple lesion—like raisin roadkill—on your back. Your outrageous Halloween costume last month didn't expose its ugly threat. I can't ask you about it—you've been unconscious since I raced to Mount Sinai.

An hour earlier, I was on my way to cheer as you marched in the Veterans Day parade—our tradition starting with last year's externship. As my keys turned the second of three locks on the Greenwich Village loft door, the phone rang and I rushed back in to hear the nurse, in a sibilant Spanish accent, say you're hospitalized. When you collapsed at the Eternal Light Flagstaff in Madison Square Park before the marchers stepped off, they called—my name and number was in your wallet.

Your soft Jheri curls, coiffed like Lionel Richie's, caress my pale palm. You take inordinate pride in grooming the precise edges of your goatee. I tug down my mask and kiss your lips. First time.

July 30, 1983

At sea with conflicted impulses, I anchor against the brick wall at The Town Pump. This evening, crowds will overflow Ft. Collins's oldest and smallest bar, but the lunchtime mood is peaceful.

My fingers tap the table and I sip a Coors while waiting for my pharmacology professor. Dr. Abelman left the invitation yesterday on my answering machine. I haven't seen her in more than a year, since my Colorado State University veterinary school class moved full-time to the teaching hospital on a different part of the campus.

She sweeps in, olive-skinned face broken by an expansive, ruby-lipped smile. With a flip of her multi-hued skirt, she skips over. Heart racing and hands twisting, I admire the dark waves caressing her shoulders.

Like a Bird-of-Paradise, she nests within the opposite chair. "Faye, thanks for meeting me."

"Dr. Abelman, nice to see you too."

Her delicate hand placates my restless one. "Please call me Devorah. I'm not your teacher anymore." Hazel eyes squint and her forehead wrinkles. "How are your senior clinical rotations?"

My skin is white and freckled—quite a contrast with hers as I pull my hand away to adjust the comfort of brown-framed glasses against my nose. "I relished ophthalmology. Maybe I have a crush—the resident, Dr. Ortega, is gorgeous."

Why do I reveal that? She's not a girlfriend. As she frowns, my posture slumps.

"Is your break during fall or spring?" She ignores our awkwardness and continues the lunch catchup.

"Two externships are confirmed for the fall." Relieved to recover a professional footing, I share the details. "The first one is late August at the Centers for Disease Control and Prevention in Atlanta. While I'm there, I hope to interview for their paid two-year Epidemic Intelligence Service—EIS—on-the-job training program."

Her face is solemn. "Two years ago at his inauguration, President Reagan said, 'Government is not the solution to our problem; government is the problem.' Is this the best time to consider a federal career?"

After nodding to acknowledge her warning, Talladega 500 NASCAR engines roar through the room when the bartender switches on the TV above the line of liquor bottles.

My head leans closer and my voice rushes on. "In September, I fly to New York City for several months at the Greenwich Village Cat Clinic. The two placements will help me decide between a public health or clinical practice career."

"Any vet can be a clinician." With one hand shoving the salad aside, the other perches over my palm. "You were one of my top students, and should aim higher."

Skin flushing from the warm pressure, I brush my short hair to counteract the heat. "Not sure what you mean."

"I grew up in NYC and recommend it highly." She beams a magnetic smile. "No pets, so I'm unfamiliar with that Village veterinary practice. However, despite the federal funding cuts, my canine temocillin research grant continues for another year. The results should be informative for treatment of human infections, and our team could use one more assistant."

After taking a large swig of Coors, I brace for my refusal. She's a PhD, not a vet, but one of the few female faculty members, and could be a mentor. Working with her pulls me in a way I don't understand.

September 6, 1983

My strawberry-blonde curls are flat and knotted like the fur of a soaked Red Persian. Used to the wide-open western skies, I've never been doused with monotonous, cold autumn rain like the last two hours, dragging my suitcase on the metal handcart through LaGuardia, buses, and subways.

I stumble across the doorstep of the MacDougal Street clinic—the room is spacious. Wooden cages and tables, gigantic bags of food, anesthesia machine, xray and laboratory equipment crowd the space. And the unfortunate smell of cat pee. No separate rooms—what if an animal escapes during an exam?

You step forward, hand extended. Smooth, mahogany skin and movie star teeth. Tall, dark, and handsome—you fit that cliché to the max.

"Faye? We're happy you made it. I'm Robert." Your voice is deep and sexy, like a blues singer. Electricity sparks as our hands touch. "Not Bob or Rob or Bobby or Robby. Let's meet the staff."

Marilyn, the twenty-something Goth technician who promised a bed in her loft, tosses a bag of baked potato chips that I tear open. Then an exquisite prima ballerina glides through the front door with a yowling Abyssinian.

"Cats are never happy when they find themselves here, by car, bus, or subway," you explain. With reluctance, I put the snack down and lick my teeth clean.

"Hello, I'm Dr. Foster, and this is Dr. Simpson."

I don't contradict you, but my eyebrows rise. If you want your clients to think I already graduated, it's your decision.

"Mr. Fosse thinks Rudolph is blocked again," she says, turning to leave. "Call Bob when you have some answers."

As I open the door on the carrier, the Abby backs away, hissing. You put strong hands on my shoulders and stop me from reaching in. "Let me wrangle Rudolph—picked up a few tricks from the Viet Cong in Nam. Take the pan and gently squeeze the bladder—we don't want it to burst."

You control the animal like a mom-cat, firm grip on the back of the neck. I'm successful at the urine sample, and your mesmerizing grin returns. "Good work, Dr. Simpson. They must teach you some clinical skills out there in the Wild West. And Rudolph will dance again."

After showing me the specimen under the microscope and injecting Rudolph with an antibiotic, you pass around the mask on the helium gas used for anesthesia. Marilyn and the NYU student join in, their voices high-pitched and hysterical. I want to be 'with it,' but we're more conservative in Colorado, and I decline.

October 19, 1983

Brilliant red and gold leaves speckle the streetsides and tree limbs. October is a magical time in the City when the sun filters through the monoliths. The pervasive odor of human waste is intermixed with the musky warmth of dying leaves.

Weeks of work and learning go by in a flash. You hate surgery, so you refer clients out and I'm not getting much practice, until a Seal Point Himalayan with glaucoma embeds his nails in the wooden table, sable tail swishing. His left eye is a vivid blue, but the right one is swollen, cloudy, and draining.

The elderly owner is frantic. "The drops aren't working—Huey won't cooperate."

I stroke the beautiful cream fur and the cat warms up, shoving his smushed face into my hand. "Removing the eye is an option. The operation isn't complicated, and indoor cats do quite well with only one."

The planes of your cheeks are rigid as you touch my arm to interrupt. "However, AMC, The Animal Medical Center, is available for further clinical consultation."

The older woman scrunches her face and rummages in her handbag. "Let me think about it."

After she departs, I clean up the table, then dart a quick glance. "Sorry if I stepped on your toes mentioning surgery."

You lounge in a client chair. "Is that a special skill?"

"Ophthalmology was my favorite rotation—enucleation isn't challenging. I'll call the resident I worked with to review."

"Go ahead if the owner agrees."

My belly flutters—I can't believe you support it. What am I getting myself into? And I still need your advice.

"Do you know where I could find a prosthesis to replace Huey's eyeball and prevent a sunken appearance?"

Your laugh is benign. "Sorry, can't help. Check with AMC."

Working with you has my hormones on overdrive, but Paul Ortega's voice from Ft. Collins revs my engine. He's gracious, treats me like a colleague, and verifies that I remember the procedure with accuracy. Then I hop the subway. When the ponytailed AMC tech brings me to the storeroom, I gulp. There are a dozen size options for the small, black silicone balls. Dr. Ortega said nothing about sizes.

I lift my glasses and rub my face. "Which one do you recommend for a cat's eyeball?"

"Eyeball?" The tech sounds confused. "That's not how we use them."

Now I'm the bewildered one. "Why do you have them?"

He assesses me with a skeptical glance—apparently, I'm an out-of-town rube. "Castration makes people nervous, especially men. The guy chooses the size, usually the maximum, so his pet maintains a stud image. Or the wife sneaks the cat in and wants the same appearance as pre-surgery, so hubby won't notice."

My hand covers my mouth to hide a giggle. Must not be enough demand in the Rocky Mountains to teach us that little trick.

October 21, 1983

To celebrate Huey's successful operation, I subway up to the TKTS booth at Times Square and buy a half-price evening ticket to *La Cage aux Folles*. Later at night, after sprightly music, drag queen dancing, and warmhearted performances, I bubble with glee and head down into the City bowels again.

When I set a heeled foot on the corroded stair illuminated by a single flickering bulb, a cop across the street breaks his stride. He glowers at my youthful face and white dress baring petite gams— clinic clients think I'm in high school—and yells, "What the hell are you doing at this time of night, girlie? Want to get yourself killed?"

He's right, the transportation system and streetscapes are seedy—as I turn my head, XXX clubs are on every block. Guys on the curb lured in customers when I strolled to the subway entrance.

How else will I get home? After my first week, when a mentally ill guy impeded my way to the market, I learned to handle myself, avoid eye contact, and go around trouble.

Regardless of the risk, I continue down into the subway. It's too far to walk and I'm way too tired. In addition to Huey today at work, there were too many spays and neuters to count. You still hate surgery, even simple ones, and hid in the lounge to read veterinary journals and war novels.

Marilyn is catsitting uptown for a Broadway star, so I anticipate coming home to an empty loft around the corner from Stonewall Place, birthplace of the gay and lesbian movement. With exhaustion from the workday and late show, I pant after three flights of stairs. The door opens before I finish turning the key, then it's pushed closed from the inside.

Snuggling in my upper bunk is a priority, but the short hairs on the back of my neck bristle. With a hand on the knob, I call out through the thin wooden door. "Marilyn, are you home?"

No sardonic, Bronx response. On twitching legs while squeezing the hand rail, I slide down the stairs to the chill night air. Couples and groups drift on by, providing a comforting sense of normality. What should I do next?

I pace in front of the red brick building, pausing to lean against the ironwork. As my breath slows, I step across to the newsstand. "Can I use your phone to call the police?"

After telling my story, the dispatcher's rough voice says, "Lady, you've been robbed. Wait for an officer."

Within fifteen minutes, one of New York's finest shows up, bulky as a tank and grumpy like he needs a cup of coffee, or something stronger.

"I'm probably paranoid—not a city girl."

The grizzled patrolman shakes his head. He's working on a five o'clock shadow, and scowls. "They come in from the fire escape— you interrupted them."

I'm sweating and hang back as I follow him into the stairwell.

"Wait here," he says when we arrive at the loft door. He uses my key to unlock it, then lumbers down the hall to survey other rooms. My bunk bed is immediately to the left, and the empty binocular case lies on the blanket.

He's right.

"No one's here." His arm waves for me to enter. Drawers are open in Marilyn's room and the living room floor is littered. "Anything missing?"

While swiveling my head, I massage my neck. "Not sure, I'm visiting. My binocs are gone, but I didn't leave any cash here."

The fire escape gloats outside the kitchen. "This window isn't secure. Tell the owner to beef 'em up. Drug addicts grab enough to sell and keep going, although they can repeat if it was easy."

As he exits the front door, he turns. "You did good, kid. But watch your ass."

Robert, I'm falling for you and the kitties, but the Big Apple might not be worth it.

November 11, 1983

"Can you handle the clinic?"

You never ask me to meet the clients alone. I'm forlorn—booked for a flight to Colorado tomorrow, but reluctant to leave. Back to a student role, bottom of the totem pole.

My voice is high-pitched. "Sure, but in a pinch?"

You flash that engaging grin, and I know exactly what you'll say. "Call AMC," we answer together.

"My First Marine Division marches today in the Veterans Day parade. Come over to Fifth Avenue during lunch—maybe you'll see me. Afterward, I'll meet you here, and we'll eat out to celebrate your exemplary externship."

At our early evening dinner, the Sautéed Cervaux—fried sheep brains—taunt me from the gleaming white china. I never spotted you in the masses of uniformed soldiers, and the lunch break didn't allow time for food. I'm starving, and these glistening organs are not breaded to disguise their origin. They match animals I necropsied in Pathology, with ridged gyri and shallow sulci fissures, but lemon scent is an improvement. Broiled steak doesn't resemble a cow enough to turn me off, but the brains do the trick.

My fingers twirl an edge of the lace tablecloth as Edith Piaf wafts through the cozy rooms from overhead speakers. The flowers in the etched crystal vase are extravagant—Anthuriums, Calla lilies, Heliconia, and orchids, with a few gardenias, my favorite fragrance. The undergrad job at a florist pays off.

After you said the name of the restaurant this morning, I pulled out my one blousy, black silk frock, but I'm still a hayseed at a cotillion. Vile barely-cooked organs and muddled mind—my smile is forced when you return from the restroom.

"I couldn't spot you at the parade. When were you in Nam?"

You ease into the Parisian woven bistro chair with the air of a panther. "Sixty-nine, seventy. Fit enough after thirteen years to still wear it," you add, as you straighten your spine like a proud Marine.

"College started as the war ended, so my male classmates missed it, blessed be. Was it horrible?"

With enthusiasm, you dig into the dinner before answering. I pivot away to avoid the slices crossing your lips.

"Can I say it was good? I was crew chief of an amtrac— amphibious tractor—hauling grunts and supplies, plus guard duty south of Da Nang. Made a man out of me, and my Dad was proud."

My unbidden thought is, *Did you kill anybody?* I'm not confident enough to let it slip. "Did it disrupt your education?"

He waves the silver fork with a chunk of brain in front of my face. "Not hungry, or a chicken-livered coward?"

I lie. "Sorry, snacked all day. Where did you go to vet school?"

"Tuskegee, for undergrad, too, interrupted by eighteen months of service. I was the first in my family to attempt college, and struggled with pre-vet courses. After failing organic chem, I dropped out and enlisted as an alternative to the Army draft. Wanted to be a jarhead like Dad."

Asparagus melts in my mouth, and the rice mixture has a piquant, salty bite. I ignore the brains. "How did you end up owning the Cat Clinic?"

"After Southeast Asia, I had to get the hell out of Alabama—the world is a wonderful and wild place. This Modern Gomorrah appeals to my need for adventure. AMC offered an internship and residency. Within two years, the clinic was for sale, so I got a huge loan and bought it."

Your bass voice sounds amused. "Never thought I'd specialize in felids, but I relate to their high-horse edginess."

My lips release a deep sigh. "I'll miss spending so much time with them." And you, too, barrels through my consciousness.

"Are you considering clinical work?"

Not a job offer—you're more direct. But reserved—before tonight, I never heard of your family or where you're from. You never mention friends or someone you're dating.

Setting my fork on the plate, I toss out a lure. "Cat practices are in large cities, which aren't welcoming to a single female from Colorado's eastern plains. There was the burglary last week at Marilyn's. And I almost got arrested on a Boston *Salmonella* outbreak during my CDC externship in late August."

"Do tell, girl." Your long body is more relaxed here, compared to the clinic. Navy blue-clad limbs stretch into the aisle on the shiny black-and-white tiled floor.

"On a Saturday, when we finished our hospital calls to find more cases, we pushed at the doors in the downtown health office building. They were locked and set off a blaring alarm. We had no luck at reaching any local colleagues at home."

"Boston cops answer the alarm?"

"They pounded on the outer glass doors, screamed their lungs out, and aimed their guns. I couldn't make out words, but the blood vessels exploding out of their florid faces had clear meaning. We were dressed casual and one guy was a Black dude, like you. Not sure if that made a difference, but they sure were apoplectic about three young people locked in a building."

You hold up a hand, with elegance, to summon the waiter. Beignets and berries for dessert—those I can eat. The offending brains vanish.

After a few bites, you ask me to complete my Boston saga. "So when's the 'almost arrested' part?"

"We called police headquarters, who couldn't locate the building owner in Cape Cod. So they ordered us to find an open window."

"Now this is getting scary." Your eyes are merry, faint laugh lines at the corners, as you enjoy my distress.

"When we shouted from a fourth floor window, a fire truck clanged up under us. Crawling on the shaky, extended yellow ladder, with no safety harness—that was terrifying."

"And at the bottom?"

"Seven o'clock, eerie evening, beefy cops scrutinizing our drivers' licenses and CDC IDs. The curious crowd was scantily clad, like call girls or drag queens. I heard a sigh of disappointment when we weren't arrested, although a few applauded. Found out the area is the red light district—hookers galore." I grimace in disgust—my church says they'll suffer eternal damnation.

Your lips turn down and you lean away—disappointed in my story ending. How did I offend you?

After signaling for the check, you examine each flower stem. "So we're too exciting here in the city."

"CDC needs to confirm if I can join the two-year EIS training program—primarily for physicians so it's hard for vets to get in. I don't have any clinical offers."

Unlike you, I'm not straightforward—my fingers are crossed that you'll know I'm fishing.

October 31, 1984

You promised to meet after the Village Halloween parade. I caught a bit of it last year during my externship, but was queasy with its vulgar excess. I'm still a Broadway fan, and the dazzling gay characters on the stage are delightful, but safely distant. For the green extern I used to be, the flashing bare skin and bawdy posturing in the parade was too much. This year is better—one year wiser and removed from my Pentecostal upbringing in Greeley, Colorado.

Under the massive Washington Square marble arch, I huddle and shiver—should have worn a warmer coat than my dungaree jacket. The air is fresh and sharp after the misty rain cleaned the streets this afternoon.

Drag queens swarm the park—I've never seen so many glamorous girls. A Nubian princess slinks toward me. She's draped in a golden gown, short enough to reveal shimmering tights on shapely legs above six-inch spikes. Cascades of thick artificial blonde hair stream front and back over her shoulders to her waist. The dress is cut low to expose a gorgeous décolletage.

My narrowed eyes move upward to full, iridescent green lips with gold moles attached at each side as dimples. Her eyelids are plastered swatches of sparkling green-and-white. Those inky eyes are enchanting—and you extend your hand like a graceful swan.

"Randy Roberta, my dear, so happy to see you tonight."

We wander to the nearest dive. With a golden arm draped over my shoulder, at your six-and-a-half feet in heels and my five-foot-three, we're Lurch and Wednesday Addams, but better looking.

The Cure's *One Hundred Years* blasts from the speakers as we collapse on plush cushions. The lyrics are appropriately morbid for the gloomy holiday. I try to stop quivering as the radiance of an electric heater loosens my contracted muscles.

Your forehead touches mine and you raise your voice over the din. "What's your poison, sweetie?"

I take in the rowdy patrons and make a choice to avoid their excess. "Pepsi. After a lengthy day managing measles at the health department, I need a kick in the pants."

You clasp the young barkeep's hands in both of yours. "Make mine a Slippery Nipple, Sambuca and Bailey's." Your fingers scratch under the flaxen tresses. "Head's already killing me—can't make it any worse."

I tear at my nails—bad habit, but I'm unsure how to make conversation with this intriguing newcomer. My hand strokes the buttery leather of the stiletto tipped on the table. "Your poor feet—I can't imagine these are comfortable."

You moan and stretch one arm to rub an ankle. Your other hand caresses the shoe and holds it up to flash in the fluorescent light.

"I only wear these beauties a couple times each year, for this parade and Gay Pride in June—amazed I made it here without falling.

Taking a hefty shot of my caffeinated drink, I probe. "So this," I wave to take in the whole outfit, "isn't a frequent night out?"

"Sorry, darling. Staid and ordinary like you see me in the cat clinic three hundred sixty-three days, loud and glamorous on two. Can't risk discovery by doing it more."

It's difficult reconciling your exotic beauty with the Marine who paraded in uniform last year and the athlete who completed the marathon two weeks ago in four hours during a heat wave—me hugging you at the finish line.

Your lips come close to my ear as your slender fingers hold my chin. I'm unclear who stimulates me more, you as Robert or Roberta.

"Is this all too much, Faye, with your conservative religious background?"

We're much tighter since I moved back to NYC at the end of July after graduation and the CDC orientation in Atlanta. The federal salary is low for veterinarians, but I'm grateful to be assigned for two years to the NYC health department. Working for you on Saturdays provides a nice supplement, and a way to keep up my clinical skills. Although you've been my guest at social events, we're not dating. I wish we were, but you're too circumspect for that. Now I know why.

My skin flushes—I've been silent for minutes. I don't want you to worry that I think any less of you. "Only admiration, Roberta. I always wondered why you ignored my come-ons."

Your fingers trace my own. "Wish I could swing your way, Faye. You're too attractive not to have been snatched up by someone."

My hand grasps yours to stop its careless stroking—your touch is too tempting. "I could say the same about you, and you're older."

"Impossible—it isn't safe to be out, or committed. Could ruin my career or make me a target. You think your family and church are conservative—try being a Black Southern Baptist homosexual."

After waving at the cute bare-chested bartender, you order a second drink. Then with your next question, I'm still the cat under exam. "What's holding you up?"

We never talked so openly. Your Roberta side is easier to relate to, despite the overwhelming perfume and creepy wig.

"I spent too much time mooning over you, and the hot ophthalmology resident last year. He was helpful on the phone with the glaucoma patient, but once I was back in the hierarchy, it went nowhere."

With a paper napkin, I wipe moisture from my forehead. Someone needs to turn down the damn heater. "I should be happy he honored the informal code of conduct."

Two dancing or stumbling Broadway queens jostle our table and both drinks slosh into our laps.

"I'll walk you home," you say like a real gentleman, or gentle lady. I'm renting from Marilyn near Stonewall Place again, a convenient location for getting down to the health department on Worth Street each day.

To avoid shredding the sparkly tights on the pavement, you discretely tug them down and I slip them into my backpack. You sashay barefoot carrying the golden heels, making it easier for us to hold hands. Your nylon mane tickles the back of my hand as you bend your head.

"It's hard making relationships in a new place, but you shouldn't stay celibate. Despite what your family told you, it's not healthy."

The fog thickens, but we dawdle. The night is too romantic, like a fantasized evening in Paris. You spin me in a delicious dance by my fingertips.

"There was someone last year, when I got back to Ft. Collins."

The wig waggles, threatening to fall off, as your face lights up. "Give me all the gushy gossip."

"One of my female professors came onto me. She tried to recruit me for a research study before I did my externships here and in Atlanta. Last spring, she invited me to hikes in Rocky Mountain National Park. My final semester and exams filled most of my time, but I went along. She's beautiful and amazingly smart—grew up in Brooklyn, by the way."

"Anything happen?"

I wipe damp curls out of my eyes. "Only first base. Too creepy—the professor thing—although it's common. One of my classmates had oral sex with her advisor because he wasn't getting it in his marriage. Dr. Abelman argued I was only a couple months from the diploma, but I couldn't handle her flirtation when I was so beguiled by Dr. Ortega, and you."

We reach the front porch of my building and are inclined to prolong the evening just a bit. The lights are out on the third floor and I assume Marilyn is asleep. After squatting on the stoop, our bottoms are soaking wet. You chuckle and wrap your arms around to keep me warm.

"Maybe you swing both ways?" Your tone is encouraging, not judgmental.

"I'm not sure what you mean."

"No matter how much I love you, I'm not sexually attracted. Only guys float my boat. But some people can be excited by men and women. You know—bisexual?"

That never occurred to me, although it could explain things. My congregation preaches that gays are sucked down into hell. Will I go there quicker?

November 11, 1984

At Mount Sinai, I put the mask and glove back on, afraid to be kicked out. They allow me to stay next to your bed for hours while the lab tests are run. Three years ago, *The New York Times* ran an article about the rare cancer in homosexuals called Kaposi's sarcoma, which resembles your lesion.

Despite how close we've become, you never talk about your sexual contacts. After making plans to meet like last year for the Veterans parade, you admitted to fevers and headaches since our soggy Halloween. I assumed you caught a cold. Now I'm flattened almost on the floor with fear you might be suffering from this new acquired immunodeficiency syndrome which they're calling AIDS.

As the morning dawns stormy with streaks of lightning, I remember to call Marilyn. At my request, she uses her key to your place, but rings back at the nurses' station that she can't find information for family members or other close friends.

My watch says 11:17 AM when you stir. I dozed off—can't account for the twenty-four hours by your side. Your lashes flutter upwards, but your fearful gaze says you don't know where you are. Or you do, and don't like it. The audible beeps from your heart monitor increase, but the bouncing green light is normal rhythm, from what I remember in the cardiology lectures. A middle-aged nurse rushes in.

"He's waking up—good news." She pushes me aside to move closer to your face. "Dr. Foster, you're in Mount Sinai, and your friend Dr. Simpson is here. How are you feeling?"

"Not sure." Your speech is understandable—maybe not a stroke. Like the morning's flashes from the rocky weather, my nerves burn with joy and gratitude. I was afraid you'd never be conscious again. Medical professionals are our own worst enemies—we know too much about what can go wrong.

An older male with an imperious stride and a bristling milky mustache bustles in. He checks your vitals and asks simple questions to verify your orientation. Every word from your lips triggers a thanks to heaven.

"We've completed multiple tests, including for antibodies. I assume as veterinarians, you both know what those are."

Yeow—how patronizing. I nod to appease him.

"The antibody test to the HTLV-III/LAV virus which appears to be associated with AIDS has only been available for a few months, but you tested positive, Dr. Foster. Your skin lesion is the gay cancer—Kaposi's sarcoma. And you appear to have an opportunistic infection—there are antibodies to the protozoan parasite *Toxoplasma gondii*, probably the cause of the brain cyst."

"Brain cyst?" Your words are slower but crystal clear.

"Nurse, did no one show him the film?" She shakes her head with a fearful expression.

He jerks it from the clips and brings it close to your eyes. "Right here, you can't miss it. We need to operate."

Your chin dips—perhaps in agreement, but I don't think you understand.

The doctor seizes the nurse's upper arm and draws her to the door. "Check the schedule and get the OR ready. Make sure everyone is scrupulous about procedures—it's still not clear how AIDS is spread."

Alone again. "Thanks for being here," you mutter.

"Robert, do you want brain surgery?"

If you say no, I'll rush out and put a stop to it, at least temporarily. My mind focuses on the immediate parasite threat. AIDS is so new, there's no treatment, and an uncertain but scary prognosis.

"An operation of this magnitude is hazardous for function after you recover. You can be paralyzed or unable to speak."

Your head twists on the white pillow, and your voice is more distinct. "We shouldn't be surprised a vet's infected with *Toxo*."

I wonder if you regret eating those sheep brains last year. People ingest the parasite in undercooked meat. But infected cats shed oocysts in their feces, leading to accidental ingestion by those cleaning the litter box. Pregnant women are advised to let someone else take over the duty, to prevent severe fetal damage. How many litter boxes have we changed?

"Robert, not getting treated will be dangerous too, so I hope the nasty doc comes back with antibiotic options. As a cat specialist, you may remember that *Toxo* is the leading disease in TORCH, the abbreviation for organisms linked to birth defects."

"Not a concern of mine."

My skin feels hot with embarrassment. "Sorry, I'm not awake but racking my brain for useful information. *The Lancet* published a report of a Spanish gay guy with *Toxo*. He visited here and got symptoms like yours, before AIDS was recognized."

"But likely connected."

I stand to stretch and inhale, hoping the oxygen revives my neurons. "Last year, there was another article about patients with acute encephalitis from *Toxo*. Some were homosexual with acquired immunodeficiency. Within the past year, our CDC newsletter, the *Morbidity and Mortality Weekly Report—MMWR—*described *Toxo* in Canadian and US AIDS cases, although I think ours were hemophiliacs. Not an issue for you?"

"Dodged that bullet—healthy as a horse before this. Faye, I'm fading and the headache is worse. Can we table this discussion?"

"Yes, I want to check with your doctors."

As your eyelids droop, my fingers contact the switch. Your dark curls glisten before I turn off the light. You're gonna be mad if you can't keep up your grooming.

November 12, 1984

My health department supervisor approves a vacation day, so I'm curled up holding the phone on Marilyn's comfy arm chair with an afghan knitted by her aunt around my shoulders. I can ask for sick leave, but it's for me or family. Aren't you family?

Devorah's voice is sweet and seductive. Nobody's nerdier than a pharmacologist, but that woman's charisma never quits. I ask if she knows of new drugs under evaluation for *Toxo* in AIDS patients.

She promises to research it, and wonders if I'll visit my parents in Colorado for Thanksgiving or Christmas. My ticket for December was mailed by the travel agent, but now with your illness, everything's as evident as a black cat at midnight. I can't leave you to face this alone. Perhaps only to enlist assistance, I promise to see her when I'm back west.

Marilyn's holding down the fort at the clinic. She's checking for AMC interns to work shifts. I'm too new with CDC to accumulate much vacation time and aren't eligible for extended time off to help beyond the weekends.

I can't abandon my EIS assignment. In addition to measles, influenza is heating up—not unusual in the fall. Last week, I collapsed to the chair as my Pennsylvania counterpart described the rabies death of a rural twelve-year-old. Choking when he tried to eat, running away from the hospital.

The boy's final days were barbaric—shivering and gagging, hallucinations, and violent yelling. Hunters and sports trappers in his area clamored for prophylactic immunizations, worried about raccoons, foxes, and skunks. We have those animals in the City. But he might have died of bat-variant, and bats are everywhere, including our buildings.

Every day, my job brings something new and exciting. They need me, and I love making a difference. When working with you to maintain my clinical chops, I help one patient at a time.

But statistical skills from my University of Northern Colorado master's degree program, prior to vet school, are in demand. I can research and develop prevention and control programs—have an impact, like guidance for AIDS and *Toxo*. Should gay men give up cats, or take extra precautions with litter like pregnant women?

My day off is devoted to you. After a quick shower, I don purple pants and blazer over a colorful striped blouse. With my reddish hair and freckles on every square inch of skin, I might as well flaunt that end of the color spectrum. Your closeted flamboyance inspires me. In the middle of the day, the subway isn't crowded as I navigate back up to the hospital.

The grumpy doctor isn't available. When turning down the hall toward your room, I collide with the timorous nurse, who says, "He's in surgery."

My jacket makes me hot and I yank it off, holding it with one arm. "Surgery? Not Robert."

"They consulted with Dr. Foster, who agreed to get the abscess out. He said he had a lot to live for, and wanted to get back to it."

Damn it, Robert, why didn't you wait for me? I'm giving you options, a fully-researched picture. Even Devorah committed to help. For someone who hated doing surgery, you gave into the hospital's desire for it quickly. Can we hit the brakes?

Like the physician did this morning, I clutch the nurse's arm.

Are we all overbearing with those who don't go to medical school? Full of ourselves, but what the hell.

"When did they go back—is it too late for more discussion?"

She pries my fingers away. Although she took it from the doctor in her hospital, she won't take bossing by me. "The operation started an hour ago. You're just a vet—why do you have all the answers?"

That's right, I don't have them. My mind can't adjust to this new normal in your life, our lives. No family is here, no lovers—did anyone try to reach them? There's only me.

The nurse guides me to the chair in your room, and her voice softens. "They couldn't wait. Dr. Foster's headache intensified—he was in unbearable pain. Then he became paralyzed on his right side and unconscious during the neuro exam."

All in a few hours while I was home, making calls. Why didn't anyone find me? But I was on the phone, and you were alone—I can't handle that, should never have left your side.

My limbs are like lead weights, gluing me to the seat. I drop my right hand to push myself up. "Let me call his clinic and update his staff. Some of them may want to come here."

As I pick up the receiver, Imperious Surgeon sweeps in. He pulls off his gown, cap, and gloves and shoves them to the nurse. "Dr. Simpson, I'm glad you're here. Dr. Foster seized, and we lost all brain activity. He didn't make it."

No, not you. No one is more in love with life—this disease can't take you away from the world, and me. Your cats can't kill you.

MERS

This is an additional Faye Simpson prequel for the alphabetical novels, not previously released.

Prologue: The Straw

In Islam, Allah has ninety-nine names, with a hundredth known only to camels, who always have a sly smile. Able to labor for days without food or water, nothing fazes them, until the straw that broke the camel's back. A coronavirus, MERS-CoV, was identified through antibodies in dromedary blood samples from East Africa. But the closest viruses are in bats from Sub-Saharan Africa. How did the microbes reach the horses designed by a committee?

Chapter One

Manhattan, New York—Friday, November 1, 2013

A thump on her chest provoked Faye to open her eyes. The full weight and all four paws of a miniature panther compressed her breastbone and the thick neck nuzzled her ear. How appropriate to wake up in an unfamiliar apartment with a black cat on a groggy Friday morning after the Village Halloween parade. Her aging muscles ached with the unaccustomed activity. She allowed her eyes to drift closed again, lulled by the animal's head butts and sonorous purrs.

Sharp claws dug into her breasts when the feline began to knead, and she nudged it to her side. Did she remember to ask for the day off work? Too many shots of Absolut Tune to think clearly. But she celebrated the iconic New York City tradition with a vengeance every year. No way she forgot to request a vacation day from the health department.

For three decades, she tried to alter the ending in her mind for the vivid night when Robert transformed to Randy Roberta and shut down Faye's romantic pass. Her overindulgence was intended to obliterate the even more horrible anniversary of his collapse while marching with his Marine unit in the Veterans Day parade. He'd been a vibrant veterinarian, too young for assassination by AIDS and a brain parasite.

An ebony leg sheathed in torn silver pantyhose moved over Faye's pale knees, and she raised her eyes to the intriguing face of the overnight partner who didn't turn her down. Taylor, a fitting name for someone in transition. Didn't have to change it.

Faye knew she was unlikely to see Taylor again. At least, that was her pattern. Consummate a hookup to capture what never happened with Robert because he'd been a hundred percent gay. Struggling to establish his cat clinic in the early eighties, he let his freak flag fly only once or twice a year. Robert loved her, but she was the wrong gender. Maybe the wrong race too, but he was dead before they discussed the intricacies of his sexual preferences.

Robert's devotion and perception left a legacy. He helped her figure out she was attracted to men and women, apostasy for a Pentecostal raised on the Rockies' eastern plains. But no one of any gender identity measured up to his wit and intelligence, at least long-term. Her sultry pharmacology professor came close but she lived eighteen hundred miles away. Faye met Robert in Manhattan when an extern at his clinic, and the City's public health veterinarian job cemented her New York transplant status.

The leg across her own shifted as Taylor opened purple-painted eyelids to reveal midnight eyes. Fingernails with a fuchsia polish stroked the skin of Faye's freckled arm. Brilliant sunshine and cool air streaming through the Lower East Side co op window highlighted her goosebumps and skin wrinkled over the extra pounds from years behind a computer chair.

Taylor's long fingers moved lower to trace the curve of Faye's hip. "Ready for round two, Bernadette?" the Tina Turner voice whispered.

Bernadette Peters, that's what Faye had shouted as her name when they met on the Broadway musicals-themed float. She studied the sculpted bronze face, uncertain if Taylor took female hormones. Faye always landed someone to assist her fantasies of making love with Roberta, even though Taylor's lower voice and lack of goatee didn't quite fit with Faye's memory of Robert.

An arctic breeze rustled a poster loosely tacked to the grimy gray wall above the double bed. Immortal Technique's *Dance with the Devil.* The 2001 rap album was famous for its violent misogyny—should have noticed that last night. Was Taylor a threat?

Faye's memories of their two AM tryst were gauzy. Taylor had not begun male-to-female sex reassignment surgery but used other body parts to bring Faye to climax. Faye lifted the flowered sheet—despite Taylor's fluorescent artificial nails, no red scratches marked her alabaster belly. Taylor had been practiced and gentle.

The kitty arched its back against Faye's shoulder, soft fur a tender tonic for the choo choo train revving up in her stomach and head. "This one have a name?"

Taylor's fingertips stroked Faye's calf to her thigh, tantalizing. "Bagheera, from the *Jungle Book.* Wise and tender, like me."

Anyone with a pet couldn't be all bad, but Faye decided to stick with her Halloween rule of fun and run.

"Taylor, you're as hot as Billy Porter in *Kinky Boots.*" Faye leaned over to caress the full lips with her own. "But you have to admit this is kinda crazy. I'm a *Little Miss Nobody* and in two years, I'll be sixty. Old enough to be your mother—thank God not your grandmother."

A pink lace strap slipped off Taylor's shoulder to a muscled bicep tattooed with a ship's anchor draped by red roses. The voice was syrupy smooth. "Bae, you fooled me. I thought we were at least in the same decade. But I won't hold it against you. I like another lady who knows what she's doing."

Faye rolled over the side of the mattress to the checkerboard linoleum, bumping the cat. She stretched toward the folding chair and the sequined green dress, chosen to complement her strawberry-blonde curls. She tugged it on, remembering her lack of underwear.

"I'm sorry, Taylor, this *Broadway Baby* is a fan of one-night stands." She spotted her matching three-inch sparkly heels and slipped them on. "You're special and I hope you never forget that. But I need to feed my Russian Blue who is likely yowling for a canned breakfast by now."

In a few seconds, Faye loosened the deadbolt and slid into the gloomy hallway, unable to hear if Taylor pled for her to stay. Two flights down, she burst into the morning's glory. A three-foot ripped gold crown and smushed hot dogs splotched the sidewalk, but colder temps damped any odor. She shivered and rubbed her arms. Stupid to assume last night's Indian summer would hold 'til the next day.

Her condo was eleven blocks to the southwest in Little Italy. She pawed through the ribbed condom packets in the canvas tote, unable to find her tennies. Blisters on her feet attested to the walk in heels from the parade last night. Her bare legs shook with a gust of air and she tossed the shoes into her bag. Soles toughened from Colorado corrals and cowboy boots could handle NYC streets, as long as she was careful to avoid hypodermic needles. She broke into a lope.

Queens, New York—Monday, November 4, 2013

Faye grumbled as she navigated the subway to the offices of the New York City Department of Health and Mental Hygiene in Long Island City. She'd invested in her Manhattan digs when the agency was still downtown. Former Mayor Bloomberg pushed development in the borough, and Faye resented the commute.

Another irritation when entering the building—no private office for a mid-rung position on the public health ladder. Open cubicles flooded a scattered mind. Dr. Moshe Moskowitz stood in the door jamb of his plaque-lined kingdom, navy yarmulke swallowed by tawny curls. His name plate with "Commissioner" was visible above his head as the black shoe vibrated in impatience.

"Dr. Simpson, I realize you taking off the Day of the Dead is an annual tradition, but we could have used you Friday." Under his heavy dark brows, his blue eyes pinched.

Always the last one to leave the office, no family members to rush home to, she bristled over his objection to the personal day. Good thing he didn't know what she did with it. *The Merchant of Venice* flashed through her mind. *You speak an infinite deal of nothing.* From the front pocket of her corduroys, she drew out her smart phone and checked the time, working hard to keep insolence out of her voice. "You scheduled me to monitor the Rat Academy for the pest control professionals and I'm headed over there."

After clicking his heels, his usual tell when he was annoyed, he turned into his sanctum and perched on the executive throne. The ornate chair was carefully elevated on a small hidden platform to make him seem taller than his five feet. Faye dropped to the guest chair at the front of the massive cherry desk.

He opened a black notebook lodged under *The New England Journal of Medicine.* "Suzanne Jaworski called from Atlanta Friday afternoon and asked for your help."

His irritation dripped like a clear pottery glaze from his dark jowls. As far as Faye knew, that was his first contact with the Centers for Disease Control and Prevention since Dr. Jaworski reassigned Kathy, their Epidemic Intelligence Service Officer, to Albany. His expression clearly reflected unhappiness that he didn't know the reason for CDC's call. He resented Faye's bond with Dr. Jaworski as rare nonphysicians in the exclusive club of EIS alums.

"I'll call her right now." Faye headed for her end cubicle lined with kitten photos torn from old calendars. Unframed and haphazardly pushpinned to the fabric walls, the happy animal faces cheered her up, especially since Moshe fumed they were unprofessional.

Faye reached Atlanta in two rings. "Suzanne, amiga, what's up? Why didn't you call me directly?"

"I need to pretend I'm following protocol." Suzanne's abrasive Long Island accent was still clear after decades away from New York. "Moshe's livid over my transferring Kathy, so we'll see what you're allowed to do on this new disease."

"I'm not your best intermediary. His complaints are incessant about my outside service distracting me from veterinary public health duties. But tell me what you've got."

"Dr. Lewis from Saint Augustus Hospital has a patient with severe acute respiratory syndrome like the SARS outbreak a decade ago. We thought SARS was vanquished, so this is an emergency if that mini-pandemic's emerging from Chinese wildlife again."

"We had a handful of imported cases in NYC back then. I'm surprised Dr. Lewis didn't call us instead of CDC."

"Apparently there's a personal connection with one of our Atlanta staff. But Lewis is also wondering about MERS. As you know, the World Health Organization has been working on it for the past year."

"Middle East Respiratory Syndrome?" With rapid clicks on her computer, Faye pulled up the *Morbidity and Mortality Weekly Report*. "Your September 27 *MMWR* mentions over a hundred cases related to Saudi Arabia, Qatar, Jordan, and the United Arab Emirates. None in the US."

"Lab tests should help distinguish between the different coronaviruses. MERS is closest to European and African bats. But the patient traveled from London and doesn't meet the MERS case definition."

Faye checked the time on her cell phone. "You want me in Staten Island for follow-up?"

"Yes. I'll bring Kathy down from Albany if you need help. Under your direction, not Moshe's. Find out if the patient has an animal connection, especially with camels. If we have MERS in the US, your previous national leadership will be valuable."

"It doesn't count much with Moshe. Being a female veterinarian is a double strike. Are you gonna tell me what happened with him and Kathy?"

Suzanne's voice lowered in volume and tone. "Faye, you weren't in her supervisory loop so with confidential personnel issues, I can't bring you in now."

"I understand, just curious if we have challenges with Moshe in common. Email the details from Dr. Lewis and I'll get on the ferry."

Staten Island, New York—Monday, November 4, 2013

"Dr. Simpson, I paged Dr. Lewis for you." Then the older male nurse headed toward the central station, leaving Faye alone in the ICU room with the patient.

Tugging away his oxygen mask, the thirty-something man in the bed tilted his head and greeted Faye with a weak but welcoming Irish lilt. "I came here for a week of Broadway musical immersion." The ICU door reopened and he continued. "Hey, Dr. Lewis, who does Dr. Simpson look like?"

"Bernadette Peters," came the soft reply as Faye spun in recognition of the voice. "With a few more freckles."

Faye grabbed the door. Same beautiful black skin, but the bright makeup and long nails were gone. No pink acrylic wig, just neat cornrows stretching to strong shoulders. "Dr. Lewis, uh, Taylor? Nice to see you again. Could you remind me of your preferred pronouns?"

The physician squeezed Faye's hand. "They/them. And I didn't catch your name or preferences when we met the other night."

As a professional, Taylor wouldn't reveal the details of their encounter, but Faye cut the handshake short. "Dr. Simpson, public health veterinarian for the city, she/her." She glanced up into Taylor's warm dark eyes. "CDC asked me to stop by after you contacted them."

"Mr. Ryan has been with us since Friday morning. He presented with diarrhea, muscle pain, fever, and shortness of breath. By the time I called Atlanta, his lung function deteriorated and we started the supplemental oxygen."

"This weekend, they threatened a ventilator," the patient added. "But I rallied and fought them off."

"He's responded well to steroids. We also tried interferon alfa."

"Why did you mention MERS when you called CDC?" Faye asked.

Mr. Ryan pulled away the mask again. "After a show in London, I visited my hospitalized boyo with a broken leg." He paused for another deep breath. "Typical London weather—it was bucketing down and I caught the pneumonia. But his nurses were muttering about this Arab flu."

Faye nodded. "Taylor, have you seen the September *Lancet* article summarizing forty-seven MERS cases?"

"I was reading it over when you arrived. Most of those patients had comorbid medical disorders. Mr. Ryan's a smoker but nothing like diabetes or chronic kidney, heart, or lung disease."

Faye gripped her gown. "You should upgrade PPE from standard to droplet or airborne precautions including a mask within three feet of the patient."

Taylor brushed away a stray cornrow from their eyes. "I realize I'm spitting in the wind with the MERS idea."

"Mr. Ryan," Faye asked, "have you had contact with bats, camels, or other animals?" When he said no, she focused again on his doctor. "I'll arrange with CDC for more specific coronavirus lab testing and someone to check on the London hospital he visited."

Taylor saluted. "You're the boss. Talk to you outside?" In the quiet corridor after they ripped off gloves, short nails covered with clear polish feathered Faye's cheek. "Three days since we slept together, and I still haven't heard you sing, Bernadette."

"You've got to be kidding. Can you imagine what this gravelly voice would sound like?" Faye glanced around for other staff and put space between them. "Taylor, trans women have a high risk of assault. You can afford better—why do you have a dingy apartment with scary posters and only one deadbolt?"

Taylor straightened and towered over Faye. "You're not the only one to deceive. With my job here, it's too risky for my pickups to know where I live. So I borrow a friend's apartment, including his kitty. Anyone who loves cats can't be all bad, right? And we meet again under different circumstances. Let's start over."

Now they looked more like Robert in the vet clinic than Roberta in the parade. Both Taylor versions were compelling, but no one compared to the real thing. Like a bobblehead flicked by an invisible finger of fate, Faye's body language and then her words said no. "Sorry, Taylor, but I'd rather jump into a lake of piranhas."

Taylor's muscled frame shrank with the verbal body blow. "Fine, you can call the shots."

It was Faye's turn to recoil from her appalling joke. "Taylor, my sense of humor was cultivated by castrating cattle and consuming their cojones. Please don't take this personally, but at this point, we need to stick to MERS."

Chapter Two

Greeley, Colorado—Thursday, November 28, 2013

"So it takes kidney failure to get you home for Thanksgiving." The strident tones of Faye's mother contrasted with the demure black dress buttoned to her throat. Her silver tresses cascaded like a waterfall to her waist. But despite the rebuke, she did her duty as the family matriarch and passed Faye several slices of the turkey raised on their farm.

"Phoebe, don't put me in the ground just yet," Charles Simpson joked. "I'm not even eighty, and the Lord Jesus Christ has plenty of time to heal me."

He hadn't lost his sharp humor, one of the few traits Faye inherited, along with a penchant for hard work and a love of animals. Thank God her mother summoned her home. The flaking skin of his jowls sagged almost to his suit collar as his head drooped over the plate heaped with honeyed yams.

Her mother's leaden eyes dropped to Faye's jeans-clad leg kicked out to the side of the chair. "How many decades does it take you to learn we don't wear pants because they are immodest? No man, even your father, should be exposed to your lower shape."

Faye held a forkful of green beans from their garden. An impulse to verbally bite back overruled her hunger. "Mother, I have no makeup, no jewelry, no exposed skin." She tugged on her curly locks brushing her shoulders. "I haven't cut my hair in several years. Would you at least acknowledge I'm making a half-assed effort?"

Like a rabid hyena, her mother snarled and pounced for Faye, jerking her out of the chair. Faye bolted out to the graded yellow dirt of the four-acre plot, whittled down from the fifty acres of her youth. Now, multistory apartment buildings and ugly industrial plants crowded the perimeter like invading soulless aliens.

Three decades had passed since the drives to Colorado State University for veterinary school, and even longer since the six years of hiking a mile west to the University of Northern Colorado for her undergrad and statistics master's degrees. Maybe that's why she hated exercise. During homeschooling before college, only a few steps had transported her from the bedroom to the religious books spread out on the kitchen table and her mother's ruler enforcing study discipline.

"Dinner's awaiting." She pivoted to see her father in his walker at the screen door.

"Dad, go back and enjoy yours. I'll be right there."

Leaning on the rickety fence rail, the sole reminder of multiple horse corrals, she mourned the loss of gentle noses bumping her hand for a carrot. Breeding and training the golden, placid Belgians, advertising symbol of the Coors Brewery, had been joy, not work.

But then the evil Big Apple lured her east for the cat practice externship with Robert, followed by two years of CDC training with the City health department, and she never left. She blessed the stars for the consequential escape, a chance to be her own person, not governed by religious dogma that condemned her to Hades for whom she loved.

At the chicken coop, she bumped aside a glossy black Australorp hen from its nest to palm an egg. No more sheep for wool, pigs for bacon, or cats for rodent control, but the pleasant clucks lured her parents out daily from the darkened home with the blinds always drawn.

It wasn't Faye's decampment that finished the farm, although having no one to help as they aged was a contributing factor. The city of Greeley encroached, a metastatic cancer. Increasing temperatures and a failing well doomed their sugar beet income from the cattle feedlots.

Faye had offered to move them to a more manageable home but they refused. When the city threatened to take over the property for taxes, she arranged automatic payments from her bank account. Then she did the same for the utility bills.

In the small plot inadequately fenced against voracious rabbits, a lone browning shoot was limp on the ground. Her boot stirred the loose soil and uncovered an onion. To pull it out, she dug in the dirt, not yet frozen. No snow by Thanksgiving—had that ever happened before?

Hands full, she prodded the kitchen door open with her foot. Her parents continued chewing in silence, not looking up.

"Mother, I apologize after you went to all this trouble cooking this wonderful feast. One more egg for tomorrow's breakfast," she thrust forward her left hand, "and a Walla Walla Sweet for dinner tomorrow. Can you forgive me?"

Her dad smiled through missing teeth. "Of course, dear. Your mother forgets I dragged you outside to help me all your life. You had to wear pants working the animals and crops. No outsiders saw you, so what's the harm, Phoebe?"

Her mother took Faye's offerings and waved to the empty chair. "Eat your fill before it gets cold."

Fort Collins, Colorado—Friday, November 29, 2013

"Campus is kinda empty over the holiday," Faye said to her host as she put her Lyme disease notes on the conference room lectern.

"Vet students will show up even on the day after Thanksgiving." Devorah Abelman's animal print skirt swirled as she rearranged chairs. "Without many Lyme cases out here, they're eager for words of wisdom."

As if on cue, the door inched open to admit a student, barely visible behind a veil of black hair.

"Here's one of my best research assistants, Maya Maguire." Devorah guided her in.

When Faye extended her hand, Maya's head tilted back, revealing the eyes and face of a teenager. Faye's graduating class of 1984 had few women, let alone a person of Asian descent. Maya's return clasp was slow and weak.

Faye smirked. "Devorah was always grudging with her praise a lifetime ago as my teacher, so that's a real compliment. What's she got you working on?"

"Uh, some antiparasitics for *Giardia*." Maya's words filtered like a soft breeze and Faye leaned in closer to hear her.

"Maya's in love with her epidemiology class," Devorah said, "analyzing the *Giardia* human and animal cases for Colorado. So I made sure she attended your talk. Faye, tell her about EIS."

Faye sat in one of the chairs and invited Maya to do the same. "If you're considering a career in public health, there's no better program than the Epidemic Intelligence Service. Two years of paid training with CDC placements mostly at their Atlanta headquarters or in a state. It's geared primarily for physicians and unlike them, veterinarians need a master's degree before applying. A long road ahead."

Maya nodded but didn't answer, and Devorah jumped in. "I don't think that would deter Maya, she studies nonstop. And a prodigy, only twenty years old in her second year of vet school."

So she really was as young as she looked. Devorah broke in again.

"Of course, I'd prefer to lure her to pharmacology, just like I tried with you, Faye." Devorah's pressure didn't change Maya's flat expression.

Buzzing like a beehive with lively chatter, other students swarmed into the room. None sat near Maya.

Faye handed Maya her card. "If you ever get out to NYC, or want to know more about CDC and EIS, give me a call."

Maya brushed the hair out of her eyes and smiled. "Thank you, this is all new to me but sounds exciting, and challenging."

At the microphone, Faye kicked off her Lyme talk. "Before we discuss our biggest tickborne disease, there's a fascinating emerging zoonotic threat you probably haven't heard about here in the backwoods boonies." Faye chortled and paused to relish the audience grimaces.

"Dr. Simpson, I already told them you're of one my CSU success stories and a Greeley native. So you can't fool us with that dig."

Faye bestowed a Cheshire Cat grin on Devorah. "Sorry, decades in NYC have turned me into an east coast liberal snob. Has anyone heard of a coronavirus infection called Middle East Respiratory Syndrome or MERS?"

Laporte, Colorado—Friday, November 29, 2013

Devorah's long black strands waved in her hot tub's blue-lit water as she leaned in for a kiss. *She's in her sixties,* Faye thought. *She must dye it, except for the dramatic stripe of white drooped over her left eye. Imitating Cruella or a skunk? No, definitely more appealing.*

"Good talk, good audience." The compliment from Devorah's ruby lips was barely audible over the sound of bubbles turned up to the max. "Lots of questions, except from my oriental princess."

"Asians don't like being called oriental." Faye's toes bumped Devorah's in a playful tease.

Devorah leaned in, hands on Faye's naked waist, pulling her onto her lap. "I stand corrected." Her teeth gently tugged on Faye's ear. "But you could be Maya's epi whisperer. If she wants to go that direction with her career, she needs someone like you. Dr. Randolph, our sole epidemiology full professor, retired. Recruitment for his replacement will begin soon."

Faye put both hands on the sides of Devorah's angular cheekbones. "If you want a serious conversation about this, please cut that out." She retreated to the other bench but left her feet floating on Devorah's thighs.

"It's been five years since you came home, unless you visited family without telling me."

"I wouldn't slip into Colorado without seeing you—I enjoy our hot tub sex too much. My parents are in poor health, but they have church support, so I haven't left them totally in the lurch."

Devorah's thumbs began a slow knead of Faye's arches. "I heard Pentecostals speak in tongues—that's kind of crazy."

Faye jerked her feet away. "My parents do that, just at the church services. I hope you're not making fun of them."

"I'm sorry, no mockery intended. Do you feel guilty?"

"About what?"

"Not being a bigger part of their lives. Maybe I can use that to lure you here permanently."

Guilt and shame were emotions Faye buried as deep as one of Colorado's Cold War missile silos. "I love my job, Devorah. NYC is its own universe, and I'm the zoonotic queen. And even though our MERS was imported from London, my investigation didn't require venturing far from my comfy cave and my kitty. I hate to fly."

Devorah's foot massage morphed to a tickle and instead of flinching away in giggles, Faye sighed in contentment. "After retirement in a decade, I'll be one of those crazy old cat ladies going to Broadway shows and Shakespeare in the Park. I'll hoard felines and *Cat Fancy* magazines."

"Do your parents know about us?"

Faye pulled her feet back and rubbed her bare arms, now chilly under the clear winter starlight. "I think they guessed. But we haven't discussed it—I want to preserve some semblance of a relationship. They ask why I haven't married and I say I haven't found the right guy. That much is true."

"Still pining for your Robert clone?" Devorah rose out of the tub to balance on its edge.

With Devorah exposed to the world in all her athletic glory, Faye glanced around at the fenced backyard, hoping the neighbors couldn't see. "This year, my parade pickup came closest to offering what Robert never did. Taylor was gorgeous and loving."

She grabbed Devorah and pulled her back in, feeling more comfortable with intimacy below the water line. "Then we met again at the hospital because Taylor was the doc for the MERS case. The floor almost swallowed me—I never had my work and private life collide like that."

"Faye, everyone's better at integrating the different parts of their lives than you."

Devorah's tone was sharp, and her switch from coy to critic triggered Faye.

"I'm not most people." Faye tried to rein in her temper, porcupine quills ready to toss. "Compartmentalization preserves my sanity. Keeping an even keel at work is all I can handle. This new Commissioner is a little Napoleon. He's insecure so I cut him some slack."

At Devorah's doubtful expression, Faye splashed bubbles in her direction. "Okay, I'm an anarchist."

Devorah placed slow kisses on Faye's palms. "CSU's Provost said that faculty, like racehorses, must be coddled for maximum performance. You might be happier here in academia."

"Hah, you're just jealous of my parade pickups."

"I'm happy for you, but sad to have competition." Devorah yanked Faye into her lap, breast to breast. "I hoped my allure would entice you to stay. I haven't been waiting around, but I'd make a commitment if you would."

Faye twisted away. "Still hitting on your students?"

Devorah frowned. "That's unfair. I didn't come after you until almost graduation. Surely you didn't expect me to be celibate when you only flit in every few years."

"Of course not, and I'm having sex with other people too."

"At least you've been honest with me, if not with the people around you in NYC. It burnishes the dull dark Novembers to get annual email missives about your latest adventures."

Devorah's reflections lit Faye up like a firecracker. "And you love FaceTime chats to ask detailed questions about exactly how I did what."

"Can't help it—the characters you ensnare at that parade are vivid. Much more varied than little old me, who's only attracted to smart women. Isn't it about time that you picked a lane?"

Queens, New York—Monday, December 2, 2013

Back at her office, Faye's first call was from Suzanne Jaworski. "Your Staten Island MERS case flew home to Ireland. OIE, you know, the World Organisation for Animal Health, is handling any of his potential exposures to animals. But a researcher is looking into suspect cases at the hospital he visited, and asked if we'd like to collaborate."

Faye rocked her chair back and settled her feet on the desk. The casual posture drove Moshe nuts. But what was he going to do with an employee of multiple decades, fire her?

"I got back at midnight from a trip to Colorado. On a plane without my Xanax, I spin like a hamster on a wheel, but I'm not looking forward to taking it again. Get one of those eager beaver EIS officers or one of your more senior CDC epidemiologists."

"This is high profile. As a national public health leader, you've got clout. Being a veterinarian is a bonus. The states must be prepared if more cases show up on our shores, or heaven forbid, we get local transmission. Promise me you'll check with Moshe."

Weighted down by the CDC request, Faye meandered to the Commissioner's office.

"You're back." Moshe rose up from his elevated seat. "Rabid raccoons are attacking dogs in Central Park. USDA wants to put out vaccine baits in hope the coons will eat them, but I'm worried about kids messing with them."

Faye agreed—the baits looked like ketchup packets. "I'll call the state health department. They've been more involved in oral rabies vaccination programs and will probably give us a hand."

At the mention of the state, Moshe blanched. "I still don't understand why they get two EIS Officers and we have none."

You shouldn't have driven Kathy away, Faye almost barked. "Dr. Jaworski just called from CDC. It's temporarily quiet on the US MERS front, but she's asking me to work with the London hospital where our patient may have been exposed. We'll be better prepared if we understand transmission risks."

He rocked onto his toes, perhaps to equal out their heights. "Absolutely not. They can't have you. You're not the best person for that job, and I need you here."

"You're right, the task is no match for my incompetence." Faye stormed back to her cubicle. He argued with her all the time, but never had been so firm on countermanding her. He hadn't been Commissioner when she served as President for the Council of State and Territorial Epidemiologists, so he wasn't used to her attention being diverted to larger issues.

She tried a generous mindset. Younger men could be threatened having to supervise longer-standing older staff, especially in a political volcano like NYC. After only two years on the job, he was still establishing his authority. She didn't like to travel anyway, so his veto shouldn't rankle so much.

The phone call to Atlanta was answered after one ring. "I'm sorry, Moshe nixed the trip," Faye told Suzanne.

"Getting to be a pattern with the women he supervises. I'm not settling for it. My next call is to the Mayor, so get your bag packed."

Faye held the phone. Caught between her NYC boss and CDC, she felt trampled flat. Religious or political authority removing her free will was intolerable, but she'd negotiate a deal to her liking.

"Suzanne, mentoring students is important to me in every investigation. If I can work it out, there will be no cost to CDC."

She followed up with a call to Devorah, excited to propose a joint MERS study including student travel funded by Devorah's grant. Being sedentary and attached to her routine had its downside; otherwise why did she live dangerously with stranger sex once a year at Halloween? Not to mention the rare exotic trysts with the tantalizing pharmacology professor, like a favorite pair of heels worn only on special occasions. London rivaled NYC for the greatest city in the world, and the compelling location might offer sufficient rewards for any travel nightmares.

Chapter Three

London, England—Thursday, December 5, 2013

At nine AM, Faye perched on a lobby chair in the Southwark area hotel. She cranked her head when a man asked for her at the front desk.

"You found me." She greeted him with a handshake. Gray peppered his dark beard and mustache—she judged him to be in his fifties. The charcoal business suit was contrasted by a red-and-white checkered headdress. *My mother's tablecloth*, came the unbidden thought and her lips parted in a broad smile to counteract the unspoken insult. *A ghutra—he must be Middle Eastern.*

"I appreciate the ride, but could have found my own way."

The short, stolid body bowed from the waist and crinkles narrowed his hazel eyes as he met her gaze. "Kareem Hussain, at your service. In Saudi Arabia, we escort our women."

She maintained a smile despite her shock at being greeted by the PhD heading the study. Gratitude for his hospitality warred with resentment over his paternal attitude. She damped down a smart remark about knowing how to drive. Representing CDC on the MERS investigation in London, it wouldn't do to provoke an international spat.

Hesitating, she searched for the appropriate greeting. As a veterinarian in the UK, she wasn't entitled to be addressed as Doctor Simpson, but academic doctoral degrees qualified. "You're too kind, Dr. Hussain. On the walk from the Tube station last night, it could have been New York."

"You must be tired with your body clock saying it's four in the morning." His voice was rich like a cello. "Were you able to sleep?"

She nodded. "Not on the claustrophobic plane, but the train from Heathrow and accommodations here are quite comfortable."

"Good, we will take the Tube again, only one stop to the hospital. Your veterinary student is here. She flew all night and is already working."

With soupy fog reducing visibility to arm's length, Faye was grateful for his lead through the rush hour sidewalk and Tube crowds. In the hospital conference room, Maya Maguire's eyes were glued to the computer. Faye preened like a mother hen, proud of persuading Devorah to sponsor Maya's travel to assess clinical outcome by treatment regimen. She got lucky that Maya had a valid passport from an earlier trip to her Chinese orphanage.

"Dr. Simpson, here are the MERS cases," Maya whispered. She handed Faye a printout with an organized Excel spreadsheet of all the patients, each one in a separate row and important demographic and clinical data from the records in each column.

Faye was impressed by the girl's initiative and organization. She was clearly more than a barely-out-of-her teens vet student. Maybe there was a mind to mold.

"Both of you, please call me Faye. We're pretty casual in Colorado cow country."

"You may call me Kareem. Now I understand why you have no New York accent." He lifted one of Maya's handouts. "In addition to your patient, infections for seven hospital staff members are confirmed. Their outcomes have been quite divergent, from low fever as the sole clinical sign to the death of our respiratory therapist. We want to know why."

"Could it be dose-response?" Faye asked. "Have you interviewed the patients to determine the length and closeness of contact with other cases?"

He scanned the list. "The hospital said the surviving employees will be at work today. We have been looking forward to consulting with you."

Faye took a gulp of the lukewarm black tea to counter her daze from the time change, wondering how people functioned with frequent travel. But she had little to complain about. With the benefit of youth, Maya had come to the hospital straight from the plane and didn't appear to be fatigued, as much as Faye could discern under her mane of hair.

"Kareem, I assume you have autopsy tissue," Faye said. "Individual differences in cell receptors for the virus could influence infection rate and symptom severity."

"Yes, for the one death, but no one to compare with."

"Run antibody tests on stored sera for other patients who died within a week of your respiratory therapist. If any come back positive for MERS, you can compare their tissues. Differences may explain the clinical variation and the classification of their deaths as something else."

His smile indicated approval. "Just the kind of strategizing we hoped for. Maya, for comparison with our MERS patients, did you select control patients from those hospitalized for fever with other causes?"

Maya nodded and Kareem clapped his hands. "Good, let's get started."

Only twenty-years-old and Maya understood the need for control patients. Faye grinned at discovering a CSU veterinary clone who gravitated toward stats.

The skies cleared in time for Faye's first sunset over the Thames. Maya didn't join them. At the first opportunity to recover from her flight and a long day of data collection, she had retreated to her hotel room. Faye didn't begrudge the girl time alone—clearly the social interaction aspect of the work was a strain for her. But if she didn't learn to communicate, she'd never succeed in a front-line state or city public health job.

"Turn around," Kareem advised. "The best view is to the east."

Spotting two turreted towers with a pedestrian walkway joining them above and a highway suspended below, she stuttered. "That looks like my image of London Bridge, but we're standing on it."

He chuckled. "A common mistake. That magnificent structure is the Tower Bridge, constructed in 1894, considered our most iconic."

A boat engine interrupted her tourist mode. "I apologize that I never offered my condolences on the death of your staff member from MERS. What a tragedy, having respiratory failure at thirty-five, leaving a wife and two children. All because of his dedication caring for your index patient."

"My guest fellowship is at Kings College so I never met him."

"Your English is so proper, I assumed you were British."

"So you think we aren't educated in the Middle East." He responded with a crooked smile. "English is an important second language and my doctoral degree is from the London School of Hygiene and Tropical Medicine."

"I'm sorry." Embarrassed that her jet lag might cause diplomatic errors, she refocused by pointing at a huge triangular glass tower poking through clinging clouds on the south bank. Before she could ask about it, he jumped in with a tourist guide tone.

"The Shard is seventy-two stories—tallest building in the UK. The observation deck opened this year. If we go quickly, we'll get a view of the city before the mist socks back in. Then I'll take you to dinner and tell you more about my home country."

"Sounds wonderful."

She hugged her knee-length puffer coat tighter to counteract the Michelin Man look. But then she snickered. "As you can tell, I never miss a meal." She was never self-conscious about her weight before, and a hunky host shouldn't change that.

When the skyscraper's elevator opened to the observation level, he pointed out the extensive railyards far below, the dome of St. Paul's Cathedral, and the London Eye, tallest Ferris wheel in Europe. She stood back from the edge—the solid wall of glass engendered images of falling into a void.

She excused herself to the restroom and almost changed her mind with the toilet a foot from the floor-to-ceiling glass wall. But how often did one get to shit above the clouds?

Darkness softened the dizzy drop and memories of the World Trade Center. Her heart rate slowed at the Hutong Restaurant on a lower floor.

"I'm not too experimental with food," she said after he persuaded her to share the signature Roasted Peking duck. "But I've eaten Chinese before."

"Do you want to order a salad?"

"I'm more of a meat and potatoes gal."

"Don't let the word Hutong fool you. Even though named after Beijing alleyways, this food is exquisite."

Red lanterns glowed in the center of each table. Through the windows, the lights of London sparkled. On a December weeknight, only a few other diners shared the cozy setting dominated by a textured concrete wall, ornate oak doors, and a large dead tree trunk with bonsai-style branches.

"So you're a world traveler," she said.

He shrugged. "My marriage ended and my children are grown."

"I didn't realize Muslims were allowed to divorce." With a sudden realization that sounded rude, she continued, "Forgive my cultural ignorance."

He brushed a fold of his ghutra behind his shoulder. "We are no different, half of our marriages end in divorce. Still, males are encouraged to have four wives at the same time." He winked.

She assumed he was kidding and responded in kind. "You should have invited the ones squirreled away here in London."

"No, that's for the Hejazi elite, rich with oil money. I've had enough of women telling me what to do. Now I can travel wherever my clinical and research interests take me."

Given his hospitality, Faye was surprised by his attitude. But possibly he was more tolerant of females in his work life than in his personal one, especially after training in the West.

"What was your dissertation?" she asked.

"A comparison of pulmonary disease in urban and rural areas of Saudi Arabia over time with climate change. But my current work focuses on viruses."

"You must miss your family with so much time here in London."

"I'm flying back to Jeddah this weekend. You should come along—we're implementing a field study of MERS and animals."

She took a deep breath and gulped her water. "I only have authorization for London and I'm not an experienced traveler. A quick consult—that's what I told my cat sitter."

"Old and sedentary, eh?"

The skin on her hands flushed to darken like her freckles. With others saying she looked younger than fifty-eight, did he know she was his senior? "Of course I'm interested. But CDC needs to approve changes to my trip."

"Our Ministry of Health was notified in early November of a male patient in Jeddah. His herd of nine camels began nasal discharge in October, and he applied herbal remedies to their snouts and nostrils. He also consumed raw milk from his herd. Then late in the month, he developed respiratory illness, confirmed to be MERS."

"I didn't specialize in wildlife." But when else could she travel to the Middle East on the government's dime, with everything handled. Courage jolted her nerve endings, and she switched from water to her hoppy Yanjing beer.

"What are you thinking about for the investigation?" she asked.

"His household contacts and the herd need evaluation. Your veterinary skills will be useful, and our collaboration is prestigious for our agencies to cement bonds."

"I can check with Atlanta." Light-headed and excited, she clinked her bottle against his.

"We'll finish this nosocomial investigation tomorrow and you can let me know then." He waved over the waiter and paid the bill.

"I'm on per diem," Faye protested. "I should pay for my own meal."

He frowned and shoved her credit card back at her. "Don't insult me, Dr. Simpson. A man should always care for the fairer sex."

London, England—Friday, December 6, 2013

After completing data collection at the hospital, Kareem chauffeured Faye and Maya through frenzied London traffic to in-person interviews with patients discharged from other hospitals.

Maya collected a flash drive full of drug regimens to analyze with Devorah, identifiers removed to protect confidentiality.

Once Maya hopped the Tube to Heathrow for her flight to the States, Faye and Kareem ended the day back near London Bridge. Wandering under the high arched metal trellis of the Borough Market, they stopped for sausage rolls at the Ginger Pig.

"This will hit the spot," Faye said. "I don't need another fancy meal like last night's, although it was delicious." She also didn't want to feel indebted. "Can you recommend a London pale ale?"

"I'll find us both a Spitfire, rich fruity flavor. Alcohol is illegal at home so I enjoy it here." Kareem left her alone at the standing table next to the cheerful green pillar, pungent odors of cheese and kebabs wafting from food stalls jammed on the sidewalks. She tugged a hairband from her purse to control her curls, frizzy in the humid environment. Too disrupted from its treasured routine, her brain felt untethered like a children's bouncy castle blown by the wind.

Taylor was her first pickup to request an extension of the relationship. Then Faye's parents and Devorah pressured her to move home to Colorado. The brief supervision of Maya's work in London was a reminder that she enjoyed teaching—shouldn't she consider the CSU job? But the government role and CDC connection brought her across the pond with an attractive paternalistic physician, or just a gracious host.

Even with Devorah's financial support for Maya's travel, Faye's trip across the Atlantic almost didn't happen. Moshe dropped his opposition when CDC promised him a new EIS Officer on condition of administrative changes to reduce sexual harassment. So without official confirmation, Faye guessed at the reason for Kathy's reassignment to the state capital. She felt guilty that Kathy hadn't reached out for support, but understood there was likely shame and fear attached. Moshe might not have been the harasser and instead allowed someone else to get away with it. He was a pompous egotist, but she never heard him say anything remotely sexual in the workplace.

Kareem returned with the beers and Faye's mind refocused on her conclusions from the two days of investigation. "Maya and I completed some initial statistical analyses. That girl is sharp—she only had one stats course as an undergrad but picked up right away what I wanted. Patients were more likely to have serious clinical illness if they were a smoker or had other chronic lung diseases."

"Not surprising," he said, "but good to have it confirmed."

"And those at higher risk treated the index case before you recognized it as MERS so the PPE wasn't as rigid, or their contact was closer than three feet."

"With the time it took for initial diagnosis and moving him to a negative pressure room, I'm surprised we didn't have more cases."

She nodded. "When those antibody tests come back, we might find some hospital staff had asymptomatic infections."

"Given your lack of experience with international travel, I applaud your decision to join us in Saudi Arabia." Kareem lifted his Spitfire in a toast. "All the world's a stage, and all the men and women merely players. And one man in his time plays many parts."

"*Hamlet*—are you a Shakespeare fan?"

"We're only a few blocks from the Globe Theatre. Let's celebrate your last night in London with a play."

He didn't ask if she'd like to do it, just said they should. She was too old to be led around by the nose like a camel. But Shakespeare was a major passion. At age seven, she'd stumbled on a book of his plays in the library and finished reading them within a year, not something she publicly discussed to avoid getting labeled as arrogant.

"I couldn't take a tragedy," she warned, "after two days interviewing MERS-infected patients or the dead hospital worker's family."

He pulled out his phone. "I can check. Ah, *As You Like It*. Light enough for you?"

She couldn't fight fate. "It's only my favorite."

He disposed of their trash and led her toward the riverside. "A bit frothy for me."

As the view opened up and an icy draft blasted, she hunched her shoulders at his smug tone. "The play's more complex than that. Touchstone the clown says, 'We that are true lovers run into strange capers. But as all is mortal in nature, so is all nature in love mortal in folly.'"

His square jaw was softened by his grin. "Mortal in folly. Not a very optimistic view of human relationships."

Reflected lights in the slow-moving Thames soothed her soul. Living close to the water was another advantage for NYC over Colorado. "I have a few years on you, and decades of love avoidance."

"Well, despite the fool's prophecy, the play has a happy ending. Maybe it will improve your attitude."

When they entered the second floor balcony, he indicated the absent roof. "Very authentic to the original, so I'm glad you have a substantial coat."

Above the browning grass embankment surrounding the upper level, the fog had lifted for a rare London starlit evening. Once the play started, the stunning poetic prose, musical interludes, and colorful costumes washed over Faye like a warm sea. Both the remarkable performance and Kareem's longer-than-expected handshake in the hotel lobby left her tingly.

Chapter Four

Dahaban, Saudi Arabia—Sunday, December 8, 2013

Dark clouds gathered from the direction of the Red Sea and the wind whipped up the sand, unanchored except at the sparse small bushes. Faye hugged the black abaya closer to her skin to avoid the stinging particles, relieved to be wearing a backup pair of glasses instead of her contact lenses. With her gloves, she nudged the niqaab veil higher on the bridge of her nose.

One handler dressed in a white robe and ghutra tugged on the reins to reduce the camel's neck movement. An older man in a long gray smock and white turban lifted the animal's upper nares to open the nostril and insert a swab. A technician took it from him as Kareem made notes in Arabic and Faye took her own in English.

The first handler grinned and spoke to Kareem, who turned to Faye. "This one is highly valuable. Last year, she won a prize with this wonderful droopy nose and lips at the King Abdulaziz beauty festival."

As the animal tossed its neck and emitted a guttural roar, the second handler sputtered with a loud voice and patted the single hump. "She is not tall enough," Kareem translated. "She only won after the first place camel was disqualified because of a Botox injection."

"You're kidding," Faye said. "I guess it wasn't a happy hump day for everyone."

Kareem's eyes narrowed at her joke. "A veterinarian got in trouble for injections to make the lips and nose bigger."

"So female camels like this one can compete and win," Faye said. "How about their owners—can women show camels at the festival?"

Kareem glanced at the other team members, then quickly back to Faye. "Of course not."

Under thick, double-layered eyelashes, the camel's eyes rolled back. When it tried to bite, Kareem grabbed Faye and pulled her back. "Signs of aggression—they can kill, so we have to be careful." The handler stroked the dark brown hair under its neck and offered it some hay.

"This one will not cooperate with a blood draw like the others," Kareem said, "and with this weather, we should call it a day."

"At least the storm will cool things off," Faye said. "December, and it feels close to a hundred degrees."

"This is our second sampling of this herd, and we plan to repeat during calving season through February."

Faye studied the sky, spotting a lightning strike over the sea. "How fast will the storm move? Do you think we have time to collect samples from the three calves? They will be easier to wrangle."

Kareem spoke to the other men and they grabbed the first calf. One handed Faye a swab and lifted the short tail. Their teeth flashed as they joked and pointed to Faye. "They say that the small American veterinarian should demonstrate her skill."

She stepped up and swiped the swab in the calf's rectum. At least the animal was shorter than she was. "No problem." Her grin was invisible under the veil but the humor in her voice needed no translation as she handed the swab to the tech. "We have camels too, so it's good for me to get practice."

Jeddah, Saudi Arabia—Sunday, December 8, 2013

Refreshed from a shower in her hotel, Faye waited in the lobby for Kareem to pick her up for dinner. Fingering the coral silk abaya, she smiled as he entered in an immaculate long white robe.

"Please thank your daughter for lending me something to wear." More feminine than her usual attire, perhaps caving to Middle Eastern expectations. But the swish of the fabric was sensual and she surrendered to the setting. CDC advised respecting the norms of the host country.

"You only packed for London and she is happy to be of assistance."

"She couldn't join us?"

"Her shift at the hospital prevents it. Besides, this way I can have you all to myself."

Although they'd shared meals in London, the romantic tension amped up as they entered the hotel restaurant. Over-the-top opulence screamed from every surface. White arches with gold leaf topped red columns. Thick tasseled floral carpets draped the ceiling to meet in the center at a geometric chandelier and at the edges to a cove of gold.

"Would milady prefer the queen's chair or the couch?"

The lounge with multiple bright patterned cushions looked comfortable—too relaxing. "This chair will be fine."

She stroked its gaudy arms. "But you'll forgive me if I act imperial."

"Women should always feel like royalty." He took the chair next to her after she was seated.

"Well, at least you're not requiring me to wear a veil like earlier today. I don't know how I'd eat."

"That was for your protection. MERS seems to increase with high temperatures and wind speeds. I wouldn't want you swallowing any virus through those beautiful lips." His fingers twitched as if he wanted to caress them, but public displays of affection were forbidden.

She experienced a brief wave of gratitude for rules restraining physical contact. Taylor and Devorah pressuring for more connection triggered concerns over conflating her work and personal life. Kareem didn't even match her preference for taller athletic partners to remind her of Robert. Yet there was something compelling about his courtly manners and earnest dedication to his work. And likely the exotic intensity of her first trip overseas. Plus, there was little chance their paths would cross again, removing any fear of emotional commitment. If Kareem's flirtation was genuine, best to have it out in the open, although discreetly.

She glanced around to confirm no hotel staff or guests close enough to hear. "You can at least give a girl a drink before starting a seduction."

His thick brows arched up as he flashed a gleaming smile. "Happy to oblige. Let's start with Saudi Champagne."

Faye fingered the red rose petals covering the pink tablecloth. "I was joking—we can't have alcohol here, right?"

"It is non-alcoholic, made of apple juice, oranges, lemon, and mint. May I order appetizers?"

"Of course, I defer to your expertise."

She wolfed down the hummus kawarma served on pita bread with fried lamb and toasted pine nuts, but passed on the kibbeh nayyeh with its uncooked meat. "Sorry, Kareem, I should have warned you I draw the line at raw. Too many images of parasites."

The mention brought back Robert's death from a *Toxoplasma* cyst in his brain. They never knew whether he was infected from cat feces or the raw sheep brains they shared in a celebratory meal. But the true villain was the HIV virus that wiped out his immune response.

Kareem signaled the waiter to open two bottles of Barbican. "Don't worry, this is a non-alcoholic malt drink. And I won't be insulted if you turn down one of our dishes. Next is fattoush, a salad with sumac spice and a pomegranate syrup dressing."

Determined to match his enthusiastic mood, she flirted. "Let's skip the foreplay and move onto the main dish."

"Shawarma it is, then. The chef marinates the lamb for hours— incomparable succulence."

As they relaxed after the meal with ma'amoul cookie balls filled with dates, he finished the story of his recent Thailand investigation into deaths from *Capillaria philippinensis*, a parasite infection from eating raw or undercooked fish.

"I told you going raw was dangerous." She leaned back and adjusted her napkin on her lap.

He grabbed her hand under the tablecloth and held it. "You're right, I defer to a doctor with expertise in diseases from animals. And you shouldn't have let me go on about my job. As you can see, other than Shakespeare, I have few outside hobbies. How about you?"

"Once at a dinner party where I was the only single, a wife accused me of being a workaholic and teased me about what I did with my nights. I told her that I was good friends with my Rabbit."

His face scrunched in a frown. "You said your only pet was a cat."

She took her hand back and laughed too loud at his confusion, causing the men at the next table to glance in their direction. With a lowered voice, she answered, "It's mechanical." Scrolling her cell phone, she pulled up a picture. "For a woman's entertainment."

His eyes crinkled with understanding. "Did your Rabbit come on this trip?"

"No, I was concerned about electrical connections and luggage checks."

Under the tablecloth, his hand moved up her thigh. "I'm so sorry. Can I be of service?"

She paused. First Taylor and then Devorah—more sex in a month than she usually got in a year. But what the hell. Offers of a dalliance didn't come often to a pudgy almost sixty-year-old and she shouldn't turn down a bird in the hand, or a handsome Saudi. With a sly smile she stopped his roaming digits. "Pay the bill and let's hit the elevator."

But he tortured her with anticipation by leading her outside. With the carpet of Jeddah lights glowing behind them, the first-quarter moon hung over the dark expanse of Red Sea, above the illuminated tower of fountain with the breeze spraying a graceful arch to the south. Despite the slightly choppy water, a stream of white reflected toward them, a mesmerizing invitation.

"King Fahd Fountain, about a thousand feet, tallest in the world," Kareem whispered in her ear, but he still refrained from holding her. "Shall we see if I can equal its power?"

The cascade was visible from her hotel room balcony as they tugged the heavy blue-and-gold curtains closed. She had a moment of panic when realizing she hadn't brought condoms on the trip, but Kareem dropped one onto the end table. At her age, pregnancy wasn't an issue, but sexually transmitted diseases always were.

As she followed his order to remove her abaya while he reclined fully clothed on the bed, her skin tingled with the idea he'd been planning this. Perhaps he always had protection at the ready.

He turned the dimmer light to low, and she ignored tendrils of self-consciousness about the freckled skin sagging from her upper arms. Her breasts, although drooping, hadn't been seared by the Colorado sun and glowed softly as he drew her to the bed before removing his own robe.

The foreplay ceased as he entered her using the lubricated condom. "You're a lot tighter than other older women," he muttered in her ear as he thrust with force and speed for a minute, then shouted what sounded like "jamil" and collapsed to her side. The backhanded compliment made her gratified that a paucity of sexual intercourse and no babies had any benefits, at least for him. Some slight consolation to counter her poor self-image with extra pounds and sun-damaged skin.

She brought his fingers to her lips and kissed them, then forced them down to her vagina. "My turn." But he rolled off the bed and donned his robe without a word. The door clicked closed and she rolled out of bed in disgust. He was just a bronco buster thrown before he left the chute, or one only aiming for the golden belt buckle. She checked her phone. He had promised to substitute for her Rabbit, but didn't even last until midnight.

Dahaban, Saudi Arabia—Monday, December 9, 2013

On a searing cloudless morning back at the camel herd where sampling had been aborted by the previous day's storm, Faye insisted on more practice taking nasal, rectal, and blood specimens. For the last day of consultation before flying home at dinnertime, she had nothing to lose by being more aggressive, making sure her clinical skills improved on the trip. Perhaps she was counteracting the impression that Kareem had directed all their sexual activities the night before. Unused to a dominating man, she'd given into the moment and violated her rule of being fully in charge. His wide grin and Arabic jokes with the other camel jockeys reinforced her conclusion that her assertions of authority amused them.

When the herd testing was complete, she suggested blood samples from its caretakers.

Kareem nodded. "Good idea, but I will try it. May I remind you that as a female veterinarian, you are not to touch these men."

She knew the abhorrence about contact between the sexes in public, but the two cups of Qahwa Arabia coffee at breakfast had fired up her adrenaline. "Kareem, I've worked other outbreaks where I drew blood from people. It's a hell of a lot easier to hit a vein on a hairless arm than an animal threatening to bite you. Only issue is the burly guys fainting at the sight of a needle, but you can support them."

His fierce expression reinforced how far out on a limb she had gone. But the other men appeared quizzical and she hoped they didn't understand English well. With his degree in research and not clinical medicine, his competence at the blood draws surprised her. Perhaps like her he was more versatile than his college diploma.

"We are done here." He set the specimens in the back seat of his vehicle.

"I have one more recommendation for sampling." Faye wiped the sweat from her brow and refused to climb in. "We should test semen to rule out sexual transmission."

His hand held her door as his voice snapped. "I assume you mean the camels."

"Yes, although MERS is so new, we don't know all the ways it can spread between people."

"And how do you propose to do that?"

"We use electroejaculators in a horse's anus to stimulate an erection and collect the semen for artificial insemination. Without a need for horses to travel, the best bloodlines can be combined."

He pivoted to the camel handlers and peppered them with questions in Arabic. Turning back to Faye, he translated their answers. "A male camel mates with twenty to fifty females. These men have no access to artificial methods."

Balancing her need to contribute versus Kareem's clear discomfort, she attempted a diplomatic tone. "But your veterinary teaching hospital should be familiar with the procedure."

"The camel meat market is more than a billion US dollars. To use the Alice in Wonderland expression, we are not going to fall down the rabbit hole of MERS sexual transmission. Allegations have consequences."

"If this is an important exposure route that you ignore, other countries will blame yours if this explodes into a larger pandemic."

He pointed forcefully toward her seat in their van. "From camels? I don't think so."

Kareem was courteous on the drive to Jeddah, with no mention of Faye's study recommendations or their previous night's sexual encounter. He chatted amiably about family visits before his planned return to London for his fellowship. At the hotel, he mentioned tickets for *A Midsummer Night's Dream* after the New Year and told her, "The course of true love never did run smooth," before bowing and making a hasty exit. So she ordered dinner in her room and a four AM wakeup call for the cab to the airport.

On the long flight to New York, she fretted over their lack of resolution. Despite Kareem's warning, she intended to consult with Dr. Jaworski at CDC, then check with King Faisal University about a camel semen study. They dodged a bullet with SARS a decade earlier when it died out on its own. But SARS didn't have a popular domesticated animal like a camel to keep the outbreak going. Infected animals with human contacts would keep MERS spreading to new areas, and more people, even if they improved case surveillance and control of hospital transmissions.

Right after touching base with CDC, she'd call Devorah and Maya. Both would get a kick out of her camel stories, and she could turn Maya loose on further research into sexual transmission of coronaviruses.

On the personal front, she resolved to forget about Kareem. He was no different than her annual parade pickups, who never lingered in her thoughts. A lifetime of noncommitment wasn't conducive to falling in love, despite the heightened atmosphere generated by an escape from her daily routines.

When staggering out of the JFK terminal at noon, reeling from the fourteen-hour flight with only a short time of sleep before it, her phone pinged with a new email from Taylor.

Health department said you're returning from the MERS investigation today. Stop by next week and join me for lunch. The death of the London respiratory therapist has me focused on infection control, especially if our next patient has a worse outcome.

The memory of Taylor's creativity and tenderness in their Day of the Dead rendezvous contrasted sharply with Kareem's traditional approach. She merged business with pleasure on MERS with only partial success, but she regretted not a minute of the trip.

Who said you couldn't teach an old cat new tricks? Keeping a role as CDC's MERS Subject Matter Expert would drive Moshe nuts—one more benefit of pushing her personal and professional envelope. Century plants took decades to flower, and she was just in the right frame of mind to bloom.

Pérdida

This reverse narrative story including Faye Simpson is modified from an earlier version released in the spring 2021 issue of "El Portal Literary Journal."

Manhattan, New York City—September 5, 2019

Katie's freckled cheek is warm to my lips—then her body convulses in a massive seizure that jerks her hand from mine. As an alarm blares, Dr. Monod pushes me into the corridor and a team rushes in to save her. Hospital staff saunter by, chatting and snacking, as if my daughter's life doesn't matter. Electrical charges course through my limbs and I collapse against the wall. Then a flash of movement—Faye steps in front of me, her expression grim.

"The PFGE patterns for Katie's stool sample match with environmental and animal samples."

Her gravelly voice echoes through a tunnel as my eyes fixate on the intensive care room, but a few of my brain cells kick in. "PFGE?"

"Pulsed-field gel electrophoresis. It means we're certain where she got it."

The ICU door opens in a slow arc and Dr. Monod's dark eyes are moist. His Haitian Creole accent is soothing but the words are harsh. "I'm sorry, Marisol, we lost her. Earlier brain images showed damage and we did our best. You can have a few minutes with her."

My knees give way but Faye stabilizes me. Wrapping an arm around my waist, she guides me inside. I lie down on the hospital bed and hear the door click as she leaves.

Tugging the white sheet away from Katie's small body, I summon memories of how she looked two weeks earlier, before our world fell apart. Back then in her cozy trundle bed close to mine, no dialysis tubes supported her kidneys and no bandages wrapped her abdomen from an emergency appendectomy that found nothing.

Her skin is cool, dark curls soft, and leaden eyes a crystal blue. Today should have been her first day of school. "Hija, how am I going to survive without you?"

Manhattan, New York City—August 30, 2019

Katie's finger follows the words as I read *Miss Bindergarten Gets Ready for Kindergarten*. "Ms. Campos, I have good news and bad news."

I drop the book to the hospital bed pillow at hearing the voice. The handsome young doctor rocks on his toes near the door of Katie's room at New York-Presbyterian Lower Manhattan Hospital. Dark, trim, and energetic, just the kind of guy I'd gone for in the past before confirming I didn't swing that way.

"And you are?"

"Sorry, Emmanuel Monod, infectious disease specialist." He extends his hand. "Katie doesn't have appendicitis, but we removed it just in case."

"You ripped her open for nothing." My tone is low and curt.

His enigmatic smile fades. "Given her extreme abdominal pain and low-grade fever, the surgeon felt it was critical to rule that out. However, we now have a diagnosis. She has HUS, hemolytic uremic syndrome, due to *Escherichia coli* O157:H7."

"What the heck is that?"

"*E. coli* is an enteric bacteria, usually transmitted through ingestion—swallowing. This strain can harm the kidneys. That's the reason for her rapid heart rate and shortness of breath."

So the beep-beep of the monitor is too fast—it's not my own rampant imagination.

After moving to the opposite side of Katie's bed, he reaches for her face. She twists her head away and asks, "¿Mamá?"

"Está bien, angelita. The doctor needs another checkup. I'm right here."

"The paleness inside her lower eyelids is a sign of anemia—red blood cells breaking down." His fingers gently touch bruises on her arms and legs. "These are from blood clots."

Blackness fogs my eyes and I brush long hair back from my neck as it heats up. "How will you treat it?"

"Intravenous fluids and a transfusion. Based on her kidney function, we may need to add dialysis."

Katie probably doesn't understand what we're talking about, but her gaze darts between us and my eyes burn.

"Dialysis—you mean like old people waiting for kidney transplants?"

He turns for the door. "Let's not get ahead of ourselves. While we work this out, someone from the city health department wants to consult with you."

I lift Katie's hand and kiss it. "Mamá will be right back." The nurse nods and I follow Dr. Monod into the hall.

A tiny sturdy woman with gray-streaked red hair stands to shake my hand. "Ms. Campos? Faye Simpson. As the city's Public Health Veterinarian, I'm here to find out how Katie caught her infection."

Monod disappears and I sink to the chair. "Not sure what I can tell you. I'm not sick and I don't think our friends are, either. She hasn't been in daycare this summer because I'm an actress between jobs."

"Some coliform bacteria are normal flora in the human and animal intestines, not causing any problems—probably helpful for digestion. But others like Katie's strain are nasty. They're shed by animals and picked up through food and water, or direct animal contact. Can I run through my questionnaire with you?"

Bronx, New York City—August 27, 2019

Diarrhea odor wafts forward as I hit the Honda's ignition button to head out for a final excursion at Coney Island before the excitement of kindergarten next week. Glancing in the rearview mirror, I spot tears streaming down Katie's face. After turning off the car, I leap out and yank her from the backseat booster. We rush into the bathroom of our brownstone. She's so weak I hold her up, and blood glistens in the toilet bowl behind her bare bottom.

My arm snakes the iPhone from my purse without letting Katie go. Her pediatrician says to bring her right in. I spread a towel on the cold tile floor and lay Katie down. An unused toddler diaper from a bottom cabinet and clean clothes—she's ready for my frantic rush to the clinic. My mind obsesses as I navigate the jammed-up streets. Food poisoning? Something from the cat? Did Katie eat a toxic plant in our back yard? Maybe all she needs is antibiotics.

Bronx, New York City—August 23, 2019

A bracing breeze ruffles the curtains, countering humid heat. The corner taqueria wafts a toasty aroma.

"Mamá, play *Coco*. What color is Dante's nose?"

After adjusting the white bows at the end of her two dark braids, I turn on Disney+ to rerun the movie for the tenth time this month. These last few weeks of uninterrupted time with Katie are magical but once she's in school, I can audition for a new musical and find another lunchtime waitressing job. Money's tight but we get by.

"Mamá, where's pink?" Her eyes dart between the TV screen and the ugly dog's outline I printed from Disney's website. She takes her time coloring between the lines of his dangling tongue. So careful, unlike me.

Coco's her favorite film, probably because of my Mexican heritage and frequent visits to mi familia in Tucson for holidays, including El Día de los Muertos at Halloween. The animated animal movies like *The Lion King* and *The Aristocats* are other favorites—that's what led to Gatito, our own cuddly tabby who cruises our legs at the kitchen table. After the art project is finished, we head to the closest county fair in New Jersey.

A musty stench tickles my nose. The petting zoo is at the edge of a large open barn door, close to the indoor pens with 4H animals. Kids groom their cows, sheep, and bunnies as families stroll by, fingers stuck in cages despite the signs. A piercing peep alerts my attention to the caged Chinese Golden Pheasant with red body, yellow legs, head, and back, blue wings, and black-and-white-striped tail twice the length of its body.

The bird's beauty contrasts with the pervasive smell. Staff are cleaning, using shovels to pick up poop, rakes to adjust hay bedding, and hoses to wash away urine. But they're not keeping up enough to suit my senses, especially in the metal pen with the baby goats.

"Ex-CUSE me." Katie bumps me with all forty pounds when shoving through the swinging gate.

I lean over the fence and yell "Watch out!" when a goat's head is about to butt her from behind. Makes me nervous to leave her in there alone. When an animal lifts up to put front feet on her shoulders, she giggles. We're here for fun—I can't let my mom anxiety bleed through to her joyful experience.

Then my stomach grumbles and scorching sun absorbs through my thick hair. I should have worn a hat. Katie's been romping for an hour—how could anyone love animals that much?

"Querida, let's eat lunch soon."

She removes her hands from a baby goat long enough to fold arms in front of her chest, stamp her feet, and turn her lips down in a grimace. "I'm not hungry." She gets her dramatic bent from me, and a disciplinarian I'm not.

Too cute in her flowered blouse, orange shorts, and flip-flops. I give her fifteen more minutes to chase the animals around the ring, screaming and laughing, with hugs for each one and affectionate tugs on their ears. When she pulls a tail, I can tell she's tired and out of control. A sign next to the exit advises handwashing. She scrapes her goat-poop shoes against the lower wooden rail and wipes dirty fingers on her shorts. At the nearest faucet, they're out of soap, and she races off for cotton candy.

Manhattan, New York City—May 11, 2014

At the birthing center, my pink little creature screams from the bassinet and the nurse nests her in my arms. A Mother's Day miracle. With minimal encouragement, she latches and nurses with vigor—I'm overwhelmed with my power to satisfy her. This will be a piece of cake. The delivery last night was tough but I was so focused on the outcome, I forgot the pain within hours.

None of my family members are here, since they disowned me when I came out as a lesbian. The Big Apple corrupted me—being gay isn't acceptable for Catholic Hispanics. When they meet this beautiful doll, they'll change their minds. The first grandchild is momentous. She has a full head of hair, unlike an Anglo baby, and her skin smells like heaven. Her eyes are a sparkling blue, not from my side of the family. The color could darken, but they're a sharp reminder of her father.

He's a struggling thespian, too. We had a rowdy night to celebrate my hire for the *Hamilton* ensemble cast, but it confirmed what I already knew—guys don't float my boat. After several months, the weight gain wasn't compatible with the athletic singing and dancing, so I lost the job and never told him about the pregnancy.

This bebé is my everything, and my only thing. Probably won't have another with my age and no relationship. Who's interested in a confused, financially unstable single mom, anyways?

I call my mother from the bedside. The wonderful lilt of her slight Spanish accent lifts me when she answers. "¿Bueno?"

She blocked my cell, but the hospital number fooled her. Will she hang up when hearing my voice?

"¿Mamacita?"

Long silence, which I rapidly fill. "It's a girl, Mamá. She's named after you, Catalina. It's good luck to be a namesake for a Catholic saint."

Still no response, but she doesn't disconnect.

"Represents purity—you taught me that was important. Can you help me make it so?"

The line finally clicks. So it's me and Katie, alone, against the world. Motherhood is God's greatest gift and woman's highest purpose—that's what the priests told me. One thing on which we can agree.

Cruel, Cruel, Cruel

This story, never previously released, is a prequel to the alphabetical novels.

Tongling, People's Republic of China—October 6, 1992

Under the pale blue sky of a warm October, Li Huiping crouches low along the rutted track to grab the spiky ginger plant by its multiple stems and yank the tubular roots from the soil. She slips and falls backward, letting go of the crop to cradle her swelling belly and cushion it from the blow as she rolls sideways. Her husband, Zhang Wei, rushes to her side.

"Please be careful to protect my heir." He helps her up and brushes mud from her cheek, darkly tanned from laboring in the fields since they planted the esteemed Tongling treasure in March.

"And cover yourself. How often must I remind you?" He tugs her scarf forward over her long, greasy hair and face round like a radish. Men favor the whitest skin possible in their women but working Zhang Wei's family farm for twenty-six years marks her with the premature creases of a well-worn saddle. Not beautiful.

Without affection, he swats at her dirt-stained dark pants. "Back to work. We must get these roots stored."

She sighs, accepting that theirs is not a love match. She smiles in gratitude that he doesn't punch her like before her pregnancy.

The ginger crop this year is bountiful, providing an extra surge of joy. The annual Yangtze River flooding left the land mostly undamaged along the south bank at Tongling. She reaches into the fabric hebao on her belt to fondle the old Chinese coin with a central hole, her good luck talisman. Good fortune is not promised so she supports the Three Gorges Dam, almost four decades in planning since Mao Zedong's 1956 poem about it.

Her husband's parents are soft—they worry about displacing two million people in fifteen hundred towns and destruction of China's archeological artifacts. Li Huiping's focus is closer to home—if the dam protects their farm, perhaps Zhang Wei can relax and take time to make love with passion instead of domination and urgency.

Bump-bump-bump. The beats on her abdomen come fast and hard. Is something wrong, did she injure her child?

She lifts the long-sleeved red shirt to study her protruding stomach and the baobèi's blows dimple her belly. She leaves Zhang Wei without a word and hurries through the south-facing double wooden doors of their two-hundred-year-old home.

"Māma, where are you?"

Her husband's mother isn't in the central courtyard open to the sky. Li Huiping glances into the ground-floor kitchen, no fire in the wood stove, but the required bright red poster of Chairman Mao glows from the plastered wall. In the upstairs bedroom that visitors never see, curtains hang from the elaborately carved wooden bed. Li Huiping parts them to find the skeletal figure.

"Mā, are you all right?" Li Huiping isn't accustomed to the older woman napping in the middle of the day. Guo Yun is burdened with arthritis from the almost-fatal beating she received as a teacher during the Cultural Revolution when her professor parents were disemboweled and eaten by their students.

Li Huiping's legs weaken as she recalls her own parents being slaughtered when she was only four years old. She squares her shoulders to drive away the deaths of so many people in the name of the Great Leader. She is forever grateful for her adoption, even though they only wanted her as a servant and future wife to their son. Bending down, she shakes Guo Yun's arm.

The older woman, gray-streaked hair pulled into a rattail, rouses and draws her patterned jacket tighter.

Li Huiping tugs Guo Yun's hand to her belly. "Is the baobèi healthy?"

Her crooked teeth, yellowed by decades of Anhui Province's famous Qimen black tea, carve the cadavered face in half. "Yes, Li Huiping, he is dancing."

The tiny feet kick again in celebration of a son to fill the old home with laughter and prosperity.

January 23, 1993

The bay horse stands in the outdoor paddock with its head lowered, looking as miserable as Li Huiping feels in her final month of pregnancy. Until last week, its small ears were always set up, alert for any activity around the ginger farm. Li Huiping wipes moisture from her forehead, unaccustomed to being overwarm with the temperature close to freezing. The horse has cultivated their fields and carried firewood to heat their home for twenty years since her father-in-law Zhang Ru brought it home from Guizhou Province.

Today, Li Huiping's cramping has begun. It's the start of the Black Water Rooster New Year and the midwife is ill-favored to ride her own horse to the farm. But she owes Zhang Ru a favor and returns immediately when he fetches her. Li Huiping lowers water buckets to the ground to help both horses drink.

"Bàba, you should not have ridden our mare today," Li Huiping says. "She is not well. And my pain stopped while you were gone."

"Your husband will never forgive us if something happens to the child," Guo Yun answers, her tone imperative like a typical mother-in-law, despite their warm bond.

Zhang Ru is gruffer. "Zhang Wei's special trip to Huizhou for steamed buns, radish cakes, and sesame candy is all for you. Too much effort, I think."

Perhaps the heat pricking Li Huiping's skin is affection for Zhang Wei's dedication. In recent days with the approaching New Year and the expected birth of his son, his tenderness has improved. None of her previous pregnancies lasted this long, and the treats are his reward.

The midwife, impatient to rejoin her family for the celebrations, takes Li Huiping by the arm and guides her into the ground floor bedroom. Despite pleasure at the most joyous of Chinese holidays, Li Huiping's mood matches the dark floor tiles of the two-story white-washed home. Her husband and his parents are convinced she carries a son but there is an equal chance they are wrong. The midwife supports the conclusion of those who pay her with a wrapped root of the prized ginger, so it is four to one.

After careful examination, the midwife agrees with Li Huiping. "False alarm, she is not ready to deliver the baobèi yet."

Li Huiping adjusts her robe and urges the midwife back outside. "You have compassion for all creatures. What do you think is wrong with our horse?"

"Hearing you say it is ill, I fear to get closer," the woman says. "Thousands of horses have influenza this year, with many deaths. Has there been cough or muscle stiffness?"

Fond of animals, Li Huiping brushes the damp hair beneath the mare's mane. She will not ignore its time of need after it carried Zhang Ru to seek help for her.

"Influenza." Guo Yun tugs at Li Huiping's skirt, her voice high and alarmed. "You cannot risk your child!"

"I do not think it is the same kind we get," the midwife assures. "But the virus can spread rapidly in the air or on surfaces between horses." She turns to Zhang Ru. "Do not ride the mare again through our area until it is healthy, or I will file a complaint."

Li Huiping continues her grooming, dread pulling on her limbs as if sinking in a rice field. "Her cough comes and go but she will not work this week. She is normally quite eager to please. I thought she was showing signs of pregnancy like me, but no longer." An abrupt twist of wind prickles her neck and cheeks. Is the mare's loss a forecast of her own?

The midwife mounts and rides her gelding a hundred feet up the dirt road, then turns back for one more stern instruction. "Your mare's fever may have caused resorption of the fetus. I recommend complete stall rest, one week for every day of fever. Otherwise your mare may have a heart attack."

The departing midwife steers her horse to the side track when

Zhang Wei's blue truck sputters into the yard, rusting to the point of disintegration. *Guerin*, the Ministry of Industrial Machinery christened the brand, to celebrate the Leap Forward of Chinese production no longer dependent on Soviet imports. Li Huiping remembers Zhang Ru's pride when he drove it home decades ago and allowed her and his son to join him on a ride, the children bouncing on the seats.

But now, the imminent death of the vehicle, along with the disturbing news that their mare could have vanished her foal, leaves Li Huiping fluttery and panicked. Perhaps she should call the midwife back.

Zhang Wei's jump from the front seat holding a large pot of blooming pink flowers allays her anxiety. She doesn't often see his grin, attractive despite several broken teeth. Maybe she can parlay his unusual mood into a back and foot massage. She rubs her belly in frustration. His tenderness will come after the baiji, an extinct river dolphin, helps her sort ginger roots in the shed.

February 14, 1993

Around the four sides of the upper-floor veranda, Li Huiping crawls on her knees from one carved wooden spindle to the next, rubbing dust away from the half-dozen painted knobs forming each vertical support for the railings. Much of the original red paint is faded from decades of polishing but the splotches of color still add pleasure to the task.

Her belly is the size of a full-grown hog. Impossible, of course, but this will be an unusually large baobèi. With no pants to fit, she wears a full-length plain black dress and adjusts its hem to cushion her scraped knees. Three weeks after the unfulfilled fantasy of a tender touch, her back aches as if hit with a sledgehammer.

A sudden gust blasts a dance of dirt through the central courtyard open to the forbidding sky. Her efforts make no sense during a storm, but Guo Yun insisted. On Sunday, February 14, house cleaning is an auspicious activity and 9:00 – 10:59 an auspicious time. Committed to loving care of her home, Li Huiping doesn't begrudge her mother-in-law a reliance on Chinese astrology for timing of tasks.

Glancing into Guo Yun's bedroom, Li Huiping is cheered by the painted flowers against a blue background of the antique cloisonné clock. The black hands point to the roman numerals indicating 11:04. The older woman snores on the bed, only her sculptured skull visible above the dark blanket. Li Huiping won't wake Guo Yung from her late morning nap, but after two hours on the hundreds of spindles, the clock gives her permission to stop.

Li Huiping struggles down to the first floor, then puts her full weight into shoving open the heavy wooden front door. In the paddock, her husband and father-in-law quarrel using the loud wurro-wurro tones of the Asian Koel, the cuckoos whose males outdo each other with their calls. Each man's eyes are almost as red as the bird's. The object of their argument is the new Heihe gelding with his thick brown hair and large ears. The family needs a beast hardy enough to pull heavy loads after the simultaneous deaths last week of their mare and old truck.

Attempting to cut through the disagreement with a high-pitched, clear tone, the midwife dressed in yellow reminds Li Huiping of the dignified motherly Qingyi role in the Beijing Opera. The woman bends to rub the animal's left hock and her facial expression indicates reassurance. Good. Although they are now in a two-hour inauspicious time period, one thing will end well.

"Zhang Wei!" Li Huiping calls in her loudest voice, "please tell Zhang Ru that I will make tea if you come out of this devil storm for a rest." Her father-in-law cups his ear and Zhang Wei repeats the invitation. Another gust knocks the door against Li Huiping's shoulder and she cries out as her water breaks, drenching her red slippers. But the midwife dashes to her side, reinforcing Li Huiping's disdain for bad omens. Strong arm around Li Huiping's waist, the woman guides her through the courtyard to the downstairs bedroom. Both men hover at the room's entrance until Zhang Rhu ascends the stairs to wake his wife.

Guo Yun fusses at the midwife, hoping to delay delivery

until after one in the afternoon when the time again will become auspicious. As Li Huiping's body convulses with contractions every five minutes, she is annoyed and excited about her mother-in-law's predictions for a child born in the year of the Rooster. At least their chattering is a distraction with no one but the midwife to guide and comfort her.

"My grandson will be handsome, kind-hearted, and humorous."

Zhang Rhu joins his wife in the game. "But also honest, courageous, and hard-working. Very important for a boy."

Not to be outdone, Zhang Wei chimes in. "One of my son's lucky directions will be Southwest. Sorry, Bàba and Māma, perhaps he will leave us to work in Chengdu or Guilin."

Guo Yun clucks. "If he is forced to leave us, he could do worse. Both are prosperous cities in the mystical mountains."

In less than two hours, Guo Yun's tone alters to alarm. "Zhang Wei, your son's head is crowning! It is too soon—I was in labor with you for much longer."

A thirty-six kilo infant Southern white rhino Li Huiping saw at the Shanghai Zoo—she is certain her child is that enormous. Sweating despite the chill air and with back pain threatening to rupture her spinal cord, she just wants the infant out.

With a final scream to scare up any of the mythical baiji remaining in the Yangtze, she tightens all muscles like steel cables for a massive push.

All the blathering stops. The midwife bundles the newborn in a towel as it lets loose with a lusty cry. She hands it to Guo Yun and cuts the cord; the placenta is delivered soon after.

"Let me hold my baobèi, I beg you." Li Huiping's hands, although unsteady, snake toward her mother-in-law. Guo Yun steps forward but Zhang Wei grabs her by the waist, then removes the child from her arms. He vanishes into the courtyard.

"Where is my husband going? What is happening?" But Li Huiping guesses the answer which the midwife confirms. A daughter. Not the son Zhang Wei insists on, under government rules allowing only one child.

Within an hour he returns empty-handed, face streaked by the rain or perhaps with tears. The darkened rooms and storm-drenched courtyard are silent except for weeping even the Three Gorges Dam can't contain.

Ringer

This graphic poem authored and illustrated by Millicent Eidson is updated from a previous release in "2020 An Anthology of Poetry with Drawings by Bill Liebeskind."

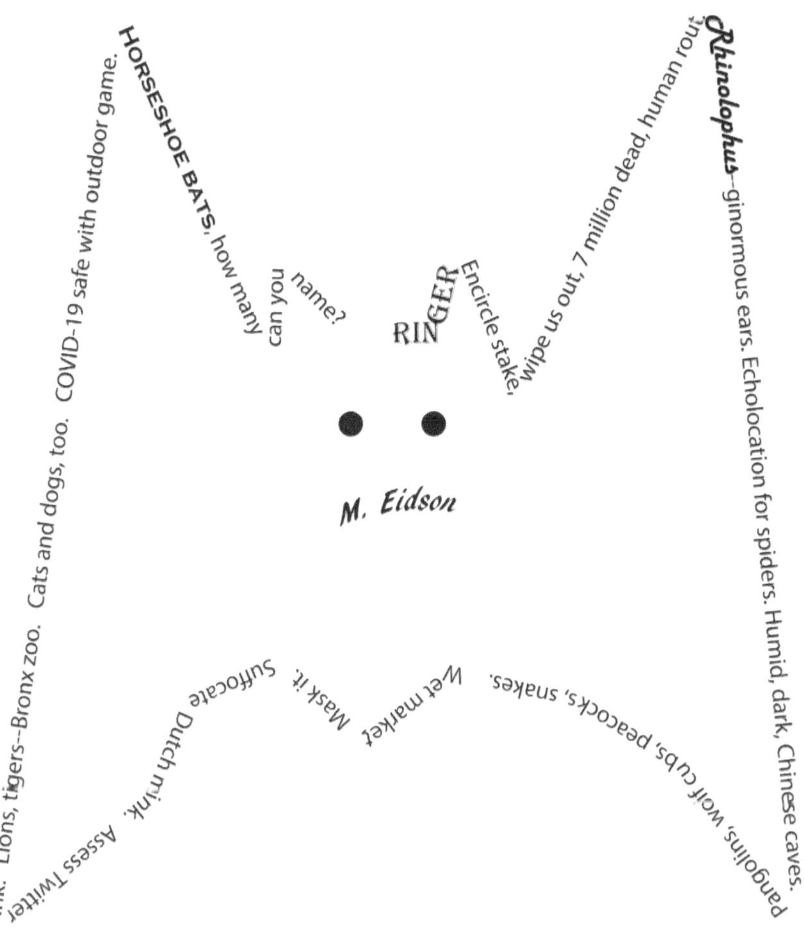

Bandit

This story is modified from 7/23/21 release in "The Chamber Magazine."

Harry despised getting up early, but if he was going to fit in a run, his jam-packed lobbying schedule required it. As he burst out of the condo elevator, he tripped over the mop bucket and his Air Jordans slid on the gleaming marble before his momentum was stopped by the glass entry door. Shaking a bruised hand, he glanced around for someone to blame.

"Fuckin' puta." The spit from his lips was aimed at a young pregnant woman, no more than a teenager, cowering on her knees with a sponge in her hand. "What's your name, bitch?"

"Dee, Denise. I'm sorry." The words slipped her lips in a whisper.

"Duh, dunce Duneze. You're gonna remember me as the guy who got you fired."

In the cool October dawn, the streets were damp from an overnight shower and slickened by colorful fallen leaves. With gentrification of the neighborhood, Harry hoped to make a killing when selling his Columbia Heights unit, but the nights remained a risk for gang shootings. Around the corner, a shell casing in the gutter and bullet holes in a beat-up Chevy confirmed noises he had heard at three o'clock.

Wiping at his brow, already beading sweat with his brisk pace, he refocused on the morning's schedule. He had to buttonhole some key members of Congress over a bill scheduled for a floor vote later in the week. If a company labelled their product a food supplement instead of a drug, the Food and Drug Administration exempted it from oversight. Some major and minor adverse health effects prompted do-gooders to argue for tighter governmental control. But thank God there were more vocal advocates on the side of the supplements, willing to pay him big bucks to maintain their market freedom.

By the time of his return to the condo, the cunt was gone. Add her sorry-ass job to the morning's checklist.

In the hospital on Halloween, a few weeks before Dee's due date, she pushed baby Jessie out. Maybe the premature delivery was triggered by months bent over for cleaning or the stress of her job loss. September a year ago had started with promise—a scholarship to Howard University. But too many tasty whisky sours at a dorm party led to this. The mewling five-pounder with the satin skin and dark doe eyes made up for all the trauma. Nursing came naturally, despite all the remembered cautionary tales from long-gone aunties in Alabama.

Harry's condo was a shrewd financial investment and place to lay his head during the DC lobbying. His real home was in the southwest corner of Virginia in the heart of Appalachia, and he hurried back there in time for the fall election. Only five thousand people, coal country, and one of the most conservative towns in the state. The hundreds of thousands earned in consulting fees paid for a beautiful old farm, which he didn't work, but the autumn-gold foliage was spectacular.

Family and friends—those words had little relation to Harry. Everyone was a means to an end. Around Veterans Day as the evenings frosted, his heart softened. When a raccoon scratched at the back door, he let it in. It was sociable—maybe others had fed it before. He scrounged under the sink for the dog bowl and stale Purina Dog Chow leftover from his coonhound dumped along a rural road after it bit him.

The coon was soft and gray, maybe fifty pounds. The ringed

tail and white-framed black mask reminded Harry of his ancestors' frontier days—didn't they brag about being descendants of Davy Crockett?

Harry kicked out his booted feet and leaned back in the hand-hewn wooden kitchen chair. He kept popular with the local citizenry by buying their craft products, even though he despised their folksy ways. Anyone who didn't spend a thousand dollars on a suit clearly didn't value themselves enough for Harry to respect them.

The ridge had record snowfall, contradicting the hysterical Dems who screeched nonstop about climate change. So Hairy, his kindred spirit, spent the cold months inside, amusing Harry by dipping dog biscuits into the water bowl to clean them with his cute versatile paws.

As Hairy chomped the coonhound treats into tiny pieces, Harry downed shot glasses of the local hooch and poured a few drops into the water dish.

"Join me, bud." He snickered when the coon lapped it up. The only heavy effort either made was Harry shoving another log in the woodstove, keeping them both toasty.

When the warmth of spring allowed outside playtime, Dee bragged to other moms about Jessie's advanced development. At only five and a half months, Jessie supported her own weight when playing in the pocket garden a few blocks from Columbia Heights Village.

Next to Jessie on the grass, Dee inhaled the floating scent of hyacinths. With her fingers, she rubbed the smooth glossiness of white magnolia blossoms dotting the area like snowdrops.

Worry fogged her mind about cobbling together enough odd jobs to put food on the table. At least she lucked out when her neighbor squeezed Jessie into her crowded unlicensed day care.

Dee's favorite time of day was bath time in the kitchen sink. She was proud of Jessie's beauty—the glistening, smooth skin that smelled like heaven and the soft dark curls. She pressed her lips to Jessie's and the baby giggled.

On the pleasant April afternoon, Harry's impatience showed with every rapid movement as he circled the Tidal Basin, Japanese cherry blossoms budding pink and purple. This was the only time of the year he enjoyed being this close to the Deep State.

When admiring a bud straight on, the vision in his left eye became cloudy, but no pain or itching. He swiped the eye and didn't feel any discharge or tearing. As he glanced around at the larger tree, there were a few white floaters. His Dad had cataracts before drinking himself to death at seventy-one. Only in his forties, Harry was way too young to have that problem, at least the eye issues.

He perched on a step of the Jefferson Memorial, clear view of the Washington Monument piercing the sky above the rippling water of the Basin and tourists whooping on paddle boats. Thumbing through the names on his phone, he located one of his White House contacts.

The guy was a special agent of the US Secret Service and they served together in Iraq before Harry was discharged for insubordination. Harry refused to implicate the guy in his misdeeds—the only nice thing he did in his life. So a favor was owed. The agent referred him to an ophthalmologist who used to be at Walter Reed before his own military service was cut short—something about harassment of an Army nurse.

"But he's top notch, I promise," Harry's comrade assured him.

Within two hours, Harry had cleaned up from the run and Ubered to one of the sprouting office towers in Crystal City. After dilation, the doc gazed into Harry's eye with the ophthalmoscope.

"No inflammation in the anterior segment or the vitreous cavity. That's good—nothing wrong with the front or middle of your eye. Let's shift to the retina at the back."

The doc adjusted his position. "Fuckin' A. Never seen one of those before."

Harry's slight drawl deepened with fear. "Hey, don't freak me out. What're ya talking about?"

"Live nematode—worm—swimming slowly in the subretinal space."

Seemingly overnight, Jessie developed a vacant stare and droopy head. At the emergency room, the doctor scratched his forehead.

"I'm not sure what it is. If infectious, she should have a fever."

Dee rocked Jessie sucking on the bottle. "But it's not my imagination."

"She's appears to be drinking well, how's her appetite?" the doctor asked.

"She still eats fine—no throwing up, no loose stools." Dee held the baby more closely. "But something's off. Jessie's different."

The intern shoved thick glasses higher on his nose. "I did a thorough physical exam. As you can see, there are no skin changes. My stethoscope revealed no gastrointestinal or respiratory abnormalities."

"There must be somebody else we can talk to," Dee insisted. She let go of her hands for an instant and Jessie flopped against her chest. "She was sitting up fine until three days ago."

"I don't have enough evidence to call in a specialist on a Friday night," the intern responded, stubbornness strengthened. He'd experienced the wrath of highly-paid superiors more than once. "I need stronger evidence to disturb them before Monday. But I can take a blood sample."

Jessie screamed bloody murder with the needle stick, oceans of tears flooding down from her inky eyes. She wasn't a hundred percent weak, requiring both Dee and a nurse to restrain her.

In the tiny apartment on Sunday, Dee covered one ear to block the fighting neighbors and held the cell phone to the other. Jessie had a high proportion of eosinophils, one of the WBCs or white blood cells, but they didn't know why.

When Dee complained that Jessie could no longer turn over on her own, they scheduled an appointment with a neurologist for Monday morning.

Back at the hospital the following day, Dee shifted her weight on the chair, unable to sit still. The plump seventy-year-old lady who introduced herself as Dr. Bautista set down her hammer. "I can confirm the reduced muscle tone you described, and decreased deep tendon reflexes."

The younger eye doctor leaned against the wall, waiting for his senior to finish. "Good news—there's no indication of vision problems when I look inside her eyes. However, she is unresponsive to tracking my visual stimuli, and there are some subtle involuntary eye movements, what we call nystagmus."

Dr. Bautista, in a grandmotherly gesture, scooped the infant up. "We'll admit baby Jessie and run more tests."

Harry's temper overcame his judgment and he shoved his eye doctor away, leaping to his feet. "How can I get a worm in my eye?"

Then he ran his well-groomed hands through thick auburn hair. "Maybe it happened when I was in Iraq. Other guys got PTSD and I landed a parasite."

His naturally suspicious mind hit pause and he grabbed the doc's white coat. "Say 'ah,' doc, I want to smell your breath. One of those three-martini lunches, and you're trying to extort me for some exotic, expensive treatments."

The ophthalmologist was equal to Harry's bluster. "Sit your butt back down in my chair, hombre, and I'll take photos to prove it to you. While those are developed and analyzed, I'm sending you to a parasitologist for blood and stool samples. If you can't poop today, maybe she'll extract a sample digitally—I bet you'd like that."

The next day was typical DC spring rainy gloom. Winds roared in from the Appalachians and scoured the cherry blossoms—tourists hit the highways and airports to go home. The National Cherry Blossom Parade was cancelled and Harry stopped back at the eye doctor's office.

"I think you're full of shit," he greeted the specialist after admiring the striking twenty-something receptionist for ten minutes. "Everything's coming back negative on my tests. But I appreciate the intro to the Korean doc for the parasite consultation. I'll give it a week so it won't seem creepy, then ask her out."

Confident of the results, he dropped back into the exam chair.

"It's morning, so presumably you haven't had those cocktails with lunch. Check my eye again and I dare you to find something."

The ophthalmologist smirked. "Sure, why not? And then I'll show you the photos of your fundus."

After adjusting the ophthalmoscope, he grinned. "Active little bugger you got there. Moved to a different spot." Before Harry could explode out of the chair again, the doc opened the screen to his laptop and pulled up the photo file. "See that squiggly little worm? Not supposed to be there."

Harry still wasn't satisfied. "Fuck it—there's no guarantee this photo is from my eye. I don't know what kind of scam is going on, but it's impossible for me to have something like that."

"You're welcome to a second opinion," the doc responded. "But I can knock it out with a laser, and the sooner the better. I'm already seeing serious damage, including optic atrophy and attenuated retinal blood vessels." He reeled out scary names for the problem—diffuse unilateral subacute neuroretinitis or ocular larva migrans.

Limbs weak with fear, Harry acquiesced. "Let's get it over with, I've no time to waste." He tilted his head up, froze his smile, and tapped the footrest during equipment prep. The laser zapped the worm with no more evidence of it on repeat checkups.

During the days after Dr. Bautista completed Jessie's neurologic exam, blood cultures and cerebrospinal fluid were all negative for any bacteria. Viral meningitis—the diagnosis of record. When the mother asked for more information, Dr. Bautista explained inflammation of the brain and spinal cord lining—a foregone conclusion with neurologic signs and no bacteria.

Dr. Bautista received approval for a lumbar puncture—sticking a needle in Jessie's spine. The cerebrospinal fluid drawn out had a high number of eosinophils, forty-five percent of the WBCs, with normal less than one percent. Dr. Bautista reflected that the name sounded wonderful in its Greek origin—*eos* for dawn and *philein* meaning to love. But the cell was implicated in a long list of nasty problems—asthma, allergies, parasitic infections, and disorders of the skin, gastrointestinal system, blood vessels, or connective tissue.

"CSF abnormalities are reinforced by other testing." Dr. Bautista handed Dee the results. "The latest blood sample has twenty-seven percent eos, when normal tops out at six."

After Jessie's brain scan the next day, Dr. Bautista reviewed all the results in her darkened office. First she slipped the CSF and blood slides under her microscope. Despite the lyrical origin of the eosinophil name, no one would dispute that they were weird. The cytoplasm, primary gel-like substance of the cell, was filled with large rough particles stained a nauseating yellow-red or orange when exposed to the eosin dye. Lobes with cell nuclei were broken up and irregular, staining dark and threatening. Of course, the strange-looking cell wasn't the culprit—just the body's response to fight off something else.

Most dramatic of all were the magnetic resonance images Dr. Bautista pulled up on the laptop. Acute demyelinating or disseminated encephalomyelitis—ADEM. The destruction of the protective myelin sheath was indicated by multiple small lesions in the brainstem at the rear of Jessie's skull. Dr. Bautista picked up the phone to summarize it for the mother.

"I'm sorry, Denise, but the scans aren't good. Jessie's body is attacking its own covering of nerve fibers. This can happen after viral or bacterial infection."

Initial treatment included an injection of immunoglobulin antibodies through Jessie's vein. But the next day, her eye movements worsened and she began smacking her lips. Her head was arched back, arms and legs thrust out, and toes pointed down. Dr. Bautista administered a steroid injection to reduce the inflammation, with no effect.

For someone so sick, Jessie kept eating, drinking, and breathing normally. But the nurses had to feed her. Dee tried to do it on her daily hospital visits, but when Jessie shrieked and pushed away, the staff took her back. At night alone in the bed they had shared, Jessie transformed in Dee's dreams to a creature out of a horror movie.

One month later, with the hospital running out of options, an ambulance took Jessie to a specialized rehab center for children. She was blind. The muscle stiffness remained and she was diagnosed with a form of cerebral palsy. Worst of all, the previously bubbly, affectionate infant appeared to have no cognitive function at all— dead inside.

Dr. Bautista could never confirm for Dee what changed her vibrant child to a conscious but uncomprehending, barely-alive form. One diagnosis was briefly discussed, with no laboratory confirmation. Neural larva migrans or NLM—invasion of the brain or spinal cord by parasites.

Dee had no clue how Jessie could have been exposed to parasites. She didn't even understand what they were. The amount of soil that slipped into Jessie's tiny lips in the park never crossed her mind. Pica or geophagia, a predilection to eating dirt—none of the health brochures at the hospital warned about it. As Dee and Jessie had slept cuddled on the single mattress, the neighborhood raccoons explored the park, helping themselves to a few veggies from the community garden and relieving themselves in the dirt.

Before Harry left the heat and humidity of DC for the refreshing altitude of the Appalachians, the Virginia Department of Health interviewed him in detail about his life and habits. They blamed *Baylisascaris procyonis*, the most common intestinal roundworm of raccoons. In the raccoon intestine, the female worm could be nine inches long as a coon pooped eggs into the soil, ready to penetrate a human's intestinal wall after ingestion and migration to the nervous system and eyes. When the State Public Health Veterinarian asked to trap and test Hairy, Harry refused to cooperate.

"At least let us collect some of his stools from the environment," the old broad begged. She could have been right—Hairy did make occasional messes inside. But Harry hadn't been home to let Hairy inside for two months, since the eye problems started. *Animal lover,* the state concluded, afraid of what the big bad guvm't might do to the creature.

The crickets chirped and bird song was muffled as low sun rays glanced through the thicket of mountain laurel and clusters of bell-shaped, purple-streaked flowers. The air was so dense, he could see water molecules dance in the light beams. At least, out of one eye. The retina had detached in the left one, and he was legally blind on that side. Taking it in stride, he thought the black eyepatch added a rakish air, intriguing to the ladies.

Recumbent on the bright blue Adirondack chair, Harry shook the plastic container with the dog biscuits. Despite months apart, Hairy scampered into the meadow as programmed. Soft patches of black and gray fur floated in the sunbeams after the shotgun blew him apart.

Eruption

This story is modified from an earlier version released in volume 188 (10/1/21) of "Down in the Dirt."

August 5, 2019

My right hand creeps up to stop the throbbing in my head.

"Vicki, STOP—you'll pull it out." The female yelling at me sounds familiar. "Doctor, what's the tube for?"

"It's a drain to remove excess fluid around her brain." The voice is male, reassuring. But whose? "We'll increase the medication dose to control Vicki's seizures."

Both voices are faint, like I'm at the bottom of a well, and there's an antiseptic sting in my nose.

"Ms. Wilkins, because she's a minor, I need authorization from her mother. Did you reach your sister in Maryland?"

Gentle fingers pull on my eyelids, which crack open to frame his black eyes, wiry handlebar mustache, and full lips. Although I'm groggy, hormones kick in. I'm hard-wired for the opposite gender.

"All right, Doctor." Now I remember that exasperated tone— it's Aunt Linda. "I'll call while you're here."

Why am I with her, and where's Jay? Oh, yeah, my brother's at Philmont Scout Ranch near Cimarron while I'm stuck in her cramped Albuquerque apartment. On a break from single parenthood, Mom's with her sleazy DC drug dealer. We're not supposed to know about him—Mom's panicked Dad will pop up from Florida and reclaim custody. But he doesn't want teenagers he hasn't seen in a decade.

"Joan, where the hell have you been? Vicki's at the University of New Mexico Hospital."

Kinda guessed that when the hot doctor said fluid and brain. My vision is hazy as he takes Aunt Linda's phone. Brown leather cowboy boots and jeans peek out beneath his white paper gown. Wild and western—my favorite type.

"Ma'am, this is Dr. Robles. Your daughter developed uncontrolled vomiting and hallucinations yesterday. At admission, she had fever, a severe frontal headache, and altered mental status. This morning, she's had several seizures."

No return conversation reaches my ears—I don't want to hear Mom's bitch voice. I'm counting the four months 'til I turn eighteen.

"On the lumbar puncture, her cerebrospinal fluid is cloudy, which means infection."

I got an A in sophomore biology, and lumbar is my lower back. He says my back was punctured—now I understand the knife blade pain there.

"We're treating aggressively—six different antibiotics. Diagnostic tests are on order, including from the Centers for Disease Control and Prevention."

Aunt Linda snatches the phone back. "Joan, get your ass out on the next flight. I'm not handling this on my own."

After hours of faint fog with shapes gliding in and out of my peripheral vision, the doctor's voice penetrates the void. "We have lab results. Did Vicki dive into warm water?"

I try to tell them about Mateo. We met last week at the pool in Aunt Linda's apartment complex while she was working. But my lips don't move.

July 31, 2019

I'm almost albino—rare flower in a Hispanic and Native American-dominated area. A gangly twenty-something leaps over my head in a cannonball, splashing water in my face. I attract tall, dark, and handsome like bees to pollen—they all want to use their tongues to suck my nectar. But pollen is the plant name for sperm— ironic.

A dormant volcano is two hours northwest. Mateo says we

can have fun and return home before my escape is detected. The pavement is rutted and slippery from last night's monsoon and the steep drop-off to the silvery creek freaks me out. I grip the truck's dash but that won't help if we tumble over. His pitbull slobbers my face with his pink tongue. I creep toward the passenger door—don't want to startle the beast and end up with jaws clamped around my throat.

After parking, we hike to the hot springs. We caress almost-empty bottles of beer—the golden liquid relaxes me for whatever is coming up. As we approach a sign, my sandals slip on loose pebbles and I bump Mateo. Both bottles crash to the gravel—what's more broken glass out here, anyways? We're alone and strip off our clothes. The dog beats us into the middle of the three pools and barks for us to join him.

Mateo tugs me in. The water is just short of burning—volcanic activity deep within the earth. He guides my naked butt between his legs as I lean back against his smooth chest. Petite ghostly feet—my favorite feature—rise up. With late August cool weather, yellow leaves waft a musty odor as they float in the clear water around our bodies. Everything's dwarfed by red cliffs topped with flaking white stone.

He waves his tanned arm through the steam. "Uh, those ginormous trees—they're ponderosa pine, spruce, and fir. The white-barked ones are aspen." *That's* all he's going to talk about?

My limbs glide around his waist when he spins me to face him, our crotches almost touching. He grabs my head and pulls me under the mini-waterfall gushing down from above. Our tongues probe as we splash, inhale water, and choke. But then he drags me out and tosses my blue jean shorts and red tee. Virtuous vaquero? Rock falls echo as a geezer couple stumbles around the corner, wheezing in the high altitude's low oxygen.

August 13, 2019

Following a week of hospitalization, I'm transferred to pediatric rehab. I could walk and talk better if only the seizures would stop.

Mom's at my bedside, her freckles brick-red, threatening to pop off her skin.

"The Santa Fe national forest sent me a photo of this warning at the hot springs. The pools are too shallow for diving, which is how most people get this brain-eating amoeba up their noses. What the hell were you up to?"

Her cell screen displays a white metal sign with bright red lettering, probably the one we passed and didn't read.

WARNING
Do not allow water to enter your nose
Naegleria fowleri
An amoeba common to thermal pools
May enter causing a
Rare infection and death

Blame it on the dropped Coronas. Amoeba sounds familiar—biology class again. Boy, did I fuck up.

Road Not Taken

This is alternative history. What might be the ripple effects if Pope John Paul II did not survive the May 13, 1981 assassination attempt? The story is modified from an earlier version released under the title "Not a Normal Holiday" in "Bewildering Stories."

Burlington, Vermont—December 24, 2020

Icosahedral gems float outside the window of my hundred-year-old home. Single-panes do little to keep out below-freezing temperatures. So I stand back a few inches despite a need for snowflake beauty.

Ten months of COVID-19 gloom isn't penetrated by Catherine Street's multicolored lights on rooftops and skeleton trees. The neighbor across the street put up an inflatable Santa but with the wind, it's hunched and deflated. On any other Christmas Eve, I'd sing *Infant Holy, Infant Lowly* with my teenagers at Christ the King – St. Anthony parish church over on Flynn Ave.

But this isn't a normal holiday—I'm alone for the first time. When a clatter of broken glass disturbs the looming silence, I turn away from my distraction with the streetside scene.

"Pepper!" Our Russian Blue leaps down from the bookcase, a guilty slink before hiding behind the sofa. Guilty as any cat can be, which isn't much compared to a dog.

The first picture I pick up from the linoleum floor is Mamá, ready to burst before my birth. She'd snuck across the border near Columbus, New Mexico after my father was executed by the cartel. Usually, women smile when they pregnancy pose in a picture. Mamá has the typical hand on her belly over the yellow-flowered skirt, but her face is lined and grim despite her youth. A small date stamp in the white margin says 1981—the year I was born, shortly after the death of the Holy Father in Rome.

I gather up the loose photos—the broken glass can wait a few minutes. After I drop down to the lumpy couch, Pepper comes out and butts her head against my arm, trying to make amends. My fingers scratch her head and the low buzz of a purr interrupts the pervasive silence. "Gatita mala." The tone softens harsher words.

I put the grainy black-and-white memorial card for Pope John Paul II in my pocket, determined to fit it back among family pictures in the large wooden frame with multiple small photo slots. Mamá was one of thousands crowding the streets when he visited Monterrey, Mexico in 1979. As a child, I stirred gumbo on the stove of our Baton Rouge shotgun home when her voice swelled with pride for the first non-Italian pope in hundreds of years and his inspiring sermons in Spanish. She was devastated when he was assassinated just two years later.

Whistling wind yanks me back to reality in a home that's spooky and too empty, other than me and the devilish cat. I head to the kitchen for a broom and dust pan. Glass and the broken frame are dumped in the trash.

Everyone featured in the photo montage is dead—is it worth finding a new frame to recreate it? Along with the photo of the Holy Father, Mamá had saved one of Papá in his mining helmet. She died too, after a deportation under President Clinton's draconian rules when she was arrested for shoplifting cigarettes. Ashamed of her secret habit, she couldn't bring herself to purchase them outright, and ended up back in Monterrey. Why did she abandon me for a nicotine addiction? When I became pregnant with Rosa, Mamá tried to sneak back north across the Rio Grande and drowned.

After brushing dust from the surface, I kiss the picture of my husband, Santiago. He died from lung cancer after fifteen years working in a Cancer Alley chemical plant along the Mississippi where we started married life. At that point, I wanted to escape anything close to the border and headed north to the other border with Rosa and Javier, my son. Vermont was known to be kind to immigrants, and Burlington soon felt like home to three Mexicans born in the US but speaking Spanish around the dinner table.

The hinge of the gold frame around Javier's soccer picture is also broken and Pepper cruising my calves doesn't ease my anger. As tears slip from my eyes, I prop the photo against a book to keep it upright.

That senile fool Pope Pius XIII who replaced John Paul II—forgive me Father for I have sinned—says that being gay is a mortal sin. No matter how far we've come on civil rights, his influence has been pervasive. Declaring one's homosexuality is a death to careers in entertainment. Even liberal leaders like President Obama opposed gay marriage. So in June when Javier hung himself in the garage, perhaps in the tiniest recesses of my heart, it was not a surprise.

I pull open the end table drawer to read his final note. *Mamacita, lo siento. I can't be what you and everyone else wants me to be. Vaya con Dios.*

What I wanted him to be? He never asked me! I didn't pick up hints when he chatted with such fondness of his teammates and never showed an interest in girls. The police scoured his laptop and confirmed he was a victim of gay cyberbullying, worsened with closed schools and online learning during the pandemic. If only he had talked to me—my love will never waver.

All summer Rosa and I mourned, wishing Javier had held on for the promise of a vaccine, presidential election, and new Pope. After all, Pius XIII is ninety-five—how much longer can he hang on?

Under his influence, legislative proposals and lawsuits to legalize Catholic mortal sins like gay sex or abortion never were successful. Maybe after the Trump debacle, we'd get our first liberal Catholic President since Kennedy. It was rumored that Joe Biden lobbied Obama to end Clinton's 'Don't Ask, Don't Tell' policy banning openly gay men in the military, but Obama didn't want to rock the boat.

At the Pope's instruction, Biden's home parish in Wilmington,

Delaware refused to serve him communion. So it wasn't surprising he lost—another four years of Trump.

Too many dead bodies crowd refrigerated grocery trucks because Trump won't fight the pandemic. I click open my computer to find an online midnight mass. Rosa promised to be home by eleven—where is she? She's always been my cross, especially since Javier died. Breaking pandemic protocols right and left. We're both young enough that we won't get too sick with it, but it's such a desolate night. Brakes squeal and I dart to the window—just a car swerving down our icy neighborhood road.

The cell phone chirps and I swipe the screen to answer it. "Mrs. Romero?"

It makes me nervous to say yes when I don't know who's on the other end, and I didn't spot any names before answering. My skin prickles with something in the speaker's tone.

"Yes, who's calling?"

"I'm sorry, ma'am. This is UVM hospital. Your daughter had your name and number as the emergency contact on her phone."

"Oh my God, has something happened?"

"Uh, she was found in a snowdrift, losing a lot of blood."

A wave of black forms in front of my eyes. "Please, can I come right over? I know you're restricting relatives because of COVID, but I need to be with her."

"Again, I'm sorry. Apparently she had an illegal abortion—she bled out and we couldn't save her."

The phone screen shatters in place of the glass I had just cleaned up as my body collapses to the cold floor.

About the Author

MILLICENT EIDSON is the author of the alphabetical Maya Maguire microbial mysteries. The MayaVerse at https:// drmayamaguire.com/ includes links to novels and shorter works. Author awards include Best Play in Synkroniciti and Honorable Mention from the Arizona Mystery Writers.

Dr. Eidson's work as a public health veterinarian and epidemiologist began with the Centers for Disease Control and Prevention and continued at the New Mexico and New York state health departments. She has authored over a hundred scientific papers, articles, and book chapters. Currently, she is a public health faculty member at the University at Albany and the University of Vermont, and teaches a UVM course on zoonoses and climate change in its Larner College of Medicine.

With formative years in the Southwest, Millie enjoys reconnecting with Arizona family, heritage trips to Norway, Ireland, and China, and wider travel worldwide. In retirement from fulltime public health work, she has settled in Vermont with her husband Tom Henderson and daughter Lian Henderson, inspiration for Maya Maguire.

Other interests are photography (website and book cover photos are primarily the author's), painting, hiking, and bicycling along the beautiful Burlington, Vermont waterfront.

Social media links: www.linkedin.com/in/eidsonmillicent
Maya Maguire Media | Facebook
Millicent Eidson (@EidsonMillicent) / Twitter
Millie Eidson (@drmayamaguire) • Instagram photos and videos

Author Notes

The MayaVerse at **https://drmayamaguire.com/** offers entertaining, educational, and enlightening insights into the mysteries and threats of microbes from animal hosts (zoonoses). Those who **join the Reader List** at this link will be sent a free thank-you gift of a shorter ebook. Links are available to novels in the series and shorter works. Publication is wide, which means the ebook, paperback, large print, and hardcover formats are available from multiple retailers. Most of these links are available at **https://books2read.com/millicenteidson/**. Audiobook versions are still in development; check the MayaVerse for updates.

The MayaVerse continues to benefit from my family team of Lian Henderson, inspiration for and feedback on the Maya Maguire character, and Tom Henderson, audio and visual media advisor for Maya Maguire Media.

Many of the shorter works in "Microbial Mysteries" were developed for creative writing classes at Champlain College and the University of Vermont. A huge round of thanks is owed to the instructors and fellow students for their inspiration and feedback. Some of these stories were also critiqued at the Burlington Writers Workshop (https://burlingtonwritersworkshop.com/), the Green Mountain Writers Group (https://greenmountainwriters.com/), and the Sisters in Crime (https://www.sistersincrime.org/) Murder, Mystery & Mayhem Critique Group.

The literary journals and websites which initially released earlier versions of the stories are listed after the title of each story. All publication rights were retained by the author.

Publication guidance was invaluable from the Alliance of

Independent Authors (https://www.allianceindependentauthors.org/) .

My continued growth is fostered by academic affiliations as an emeritus professor at the University at Albany and instructor for a zoonoses class at the University of Vermont.

Information was contributed by Kelsey Henderson. Provision of information by others including agency employees or workshop participants does not imply endorsement by those individuals or groups.

Scientific nomenclature including when to italicize organism names can be confusing. For more information, see https://wwwnc.cdc.gov/eid/page/scientific-nomenclature.

Although the stories in "Microbial Mysteries" are informed by fact, the book is a work of fiction. Descriptions of events, locations, agencies, or agency staff and functions are intended to anchor the stories in public health science and the larger world. However, the characters live in the altered world of the MayaVerse and their actions do not represent specific activities of real people or institutions.

Readers who would like to consult on future MayaVerse stories or provide feedback on "Microbial Mysteries" are welcome to email: drmayamaguire@gmail.com. **Ratings and reviews are critically important to help others discover the MayaVerse.** Share a few sentences about "Microbial Mysteries" at the retailer where it was purchased or at BookBub: **https://www.bookbub.com/welcome.**

Microbial Mysteries Discussion Questions

Book groups interested in discussions with the author should email drmayamaguire@gmail.com.

The following questions may help in thinking about and discussing this compilation of shorter works.

1. The genre elements include mystery, women's fiction, and romantic suspense. How do each of these elements contribute to the overall arc and your enjoyment of the stories?

2. What do short stories offer compared to full-length novels?

3. Is your reading enriched by the different points-of-view and style of each story?

4. What are some biological, regional, cultural, and religious influences on our perceptions of 'the other'?

5. How do geography and history influence these stories?

6. How do these stories about disease microbes from animals, many taking place prior to the COVID pandemic, foreshadow societal, medical, and public health challenges beginning in 2020?

7. Does the appearance of characters from the novels in these short stories benefit your understanding of the MayaVerse and the characters' relationships with Maya Maguire in the novels?

8. Zoonotic diseases are those in common between humans
and non-human animals. How are transmission, investigation,
prevention, and control more complex for zoonotic diseases than
those infecting only humans?

9. How can someone with a veterinary medical degree contribute
to disease investigations?

10. For authenticity, writers often rely on personal experience,
while protecting privacy of those sharing life events with the
author. Writers also use research and close consultation with
others to create characters, plot events, and settings not their own.
As a reader, do you have a preferred balance of work informed
by an author's imagination, research, and representation of their
background?

www.ingramcontent.com/pod-product-compliance
Lightning Source LLC
Chambersburg PA
CBHW031247210726
48287CB00003B/925